THE TRUTH HAS ARMS AND LEGS

ALICE FOWLER

First published July 2023 in the UK by
Fly on the Wall Press
The Wentwood
72-76 Newton St
Manchester
M1 1EW
www.flyonthewallpress.co.uk
ISBN: 9781915789082
Copyright Alice Fowler © 2023

The right of Alice Fowler to be identified as the author of this work has been asserted in accordance with the Copyright, Designs and Patents Act 1988. Typesetting and cover design by Isabelle Kenyon, imagery Shutterstock.

This is a work of fiction.The opinions expressed are those of the characters and should not be confused with the author's. Neither the author nor the publisher will be held liable or responsible for any actual or perceived loss or damage to any person or entity, caused or alleged to have been caused, directly or indirectly, by anything in this book.

A CIP Catalogue record for this book is available from the British Library.

Printed in the UK on responsibly sourced paper

For everyone who has read, listened and encouraged.

CONTENTS

THE RACE

THE HURTWOOD, SURREY, 1928

I stand, pinned, not certain if I've heard the whistle.

"Run, Mags!"

That's Jack, my little brother, startling me to life.

My eyes turn up the track. The village girls are five yards out, eating up the ground. In front is Lorrie Chandler: running like it's for England, not to put some gypsies in their place.

"Run, Maggie!"

That's my teacher, Mr. Milner, in his shirt and knitted tie. Kind, patient, never shouts. If he says go, I'm off.

I run, legs taut as rusted wire. I'm like a deer, Ma says: bounding, like I'm trying to see to the next place.

"Try your best, children," Mr. Milner told us, just before the race.

That's all right for him. He ain't running bare-foot, 'gainst them village kids in shoes. Bodies white and doughy, all flashing teeth and hair; us dark and scrawny, our limbs like knotted string.

Two laps round the track, a race for girls and one for boys. After that it's tea, to make it worth our while. Sandwiches, cakes and '*do have another*'. "You look hungry, little girl, how about one of these?" Brown bread, white bread, crusts cut off; egg mushed with something so delicious I can taste it for a year. Ladies in their dresses, giving out their smiles. The day they forget the 'gypsy nuisance' and act like we're all friends.

There's a girl not far ahead, blowing like a horse. Her shoes, black and rubbery, are flapping at her heels. Me, I like to feel the grass and stones. How can you run, if your feet can't read the ground?

Our school, it's the first for gypsies in the land. Imagine that: me, Mags Hoadley, ten years old, picked out to get some learning. Mr. Milner shows us pictures: dog, horse, tree. Next thing, we've got a board to scratch our names on. More than Pa can do, or Ma.

Pa makes out he don't like the school. Says, what do we need with reading, writing, counting? We're Gypsies. We've got more important things to know.

I don't believe him. Why else are we pitched up at the Hurtwood? Us and twenty other 'vans, nestled in the pines; going nowhere, smoke twisting from our roofs?

We ain't here to see Sir Reginald, that's for sure.

Sir Reggie: I see him by the food tent, as I run around the bend. These woods and heaths, they're his, far as any eye can see. He owns the sandy land we camp on, the water from the well; the heather and the berries, the hidden hollow ways.

Hat, moustache, round specs and beady eyes. A nose that's bigger than it should be, for poking into our affairs. "Five shillings, for a licence," that's what he told Pa. "You're a strain on resources, Mr. Hoadley. Paying up is only fair."

Fair? When he owns so many thousand acres, and we have none at all? Pa's fist twitched. For decades we Hoadleys been camping at the Hurtwood. Picking fruit, working where we're wanted. Welcomed, not made to pay.

Pa, he don't have five shillings, not that's going spare. That night, Sir Reggie's pheasants took a culling. Feathered bodies off to Dorking market; by evening, five shillings stuffed into his lordship's palm.

We're going faster now, dust rising. I look back for my friends. Jess is sitting, holding up her foot; Sarah crouched above her, like she's searching for a thorn.

That won't beat Lorrie Chandler. I'll have to do it on my own.

Jack, my little brother, he can't run ten yards without a break. His chest's too weak to run; too weak for learning, Ma used to say as well.

Mr. Milner, he don't know that. He comes up to our tent one morning, like he's feeling right at home. It's a bender: hazel poles, curved and pegged; sacks and heather over. "Mrs. Hoadley," he says, polite. "Your son needs an education. Not being strong, he will have to use his brain."

"Use his brain" — that got to Ma. She knows Jack's brain is bigger than the King of England's. Next day, Jack's up and dressed. He's sitting at his school desk doing lessons, while Pa's still hawking by the fire.

The girl ahead is slowing. I pass her on a bend.

The County Council, they've given us the school; not Sir Reggie, though he acts as though he has. Each week he comes a-rapping, peering, like he wants to catch us out. Me, I move my arm back. I want him to see where Mr. Milner's pencilled me a star.

Mr. Milner tells us stories: kings and Romans, maps of far-off lands. We teach him songs, to track a fox-cub, where to dig the ancient coins. He can't stop asking questions. "Who's teaching who?" he says.

Mr. Milner — he's by the track beside me. "Keep going. You can do it."

Can I? That's not what Ma says. Miss Fingers and Thumbs, she calls me. Not like my sisters, Bess and Annie, who work at the big house.

Me? I'm the useless one. That's what I used to think – until our school on wheels rolled up. Until I learnt to read.

I'm on the second lap now. Legs slicing, blood a-hammer in my head.

That man with the rosebud in his button-hole, that's Councillor Stone. Every Sunday, he's up here at the camp. Brings us sweets and oranges. Tries to teach us songs about fighting the good fight.

This day – this race – it's down to him. He wants us and the village to be neighbours and, one day, even friends. Sir, I think, you don't know about the 'gypsy nuisance'. You ain't seen them hold their noses, complaining that we stink.

Jack's cutting up towards me. "You can do it, Mags," he squeaks.

Ma goes to the school now, two evenings every week. Pa, he don't like it.

"All I do is look at pictures, Tom," she tells him back. "Don't do any harm."

Ma's brain's as big as Jack's, I'm sure of it. Just spent her whole life scraping cooking pots and looking after Pa.

This lap, it's the one that counts. Ahead, the village kids are throwing out their legs. There's a magic that makes each stride of theirs twice as wide as ours.

Jess says you run faster if you think of cake. I try it: all the sweet treats in the baker's shop Ma won't let us have. Once, I saw a paper bag, left outside the shop. '*Yesterday's: 2d: for the birds*', in pencil on the side.

My brain added more words: 'For the birds, or the gypsies, or whoever else is hungry'. Quick as a flash, I grabbed it and set off up the street. Too slow, for next thing there's a holler: "Thieving gypsy! Give that back!"

I ran, o' course, fast as I am now. Didn't know hidden eyes were watching. Didn't know Pa would hear of it and thrash me, so hard I couldn't walk.

She's tiring, the girl ahead: shoes scuffing. I move out wide. Then I'm past her and away, toes splayed out in triumph. If I keep going, I'll be third.

Third! Third means a rosette. No gypsy's ever won one. That's against the rules.

Breath comes at my shoulder. While I've been dreaming, that girl's been catching up.

"Magg-ie!"

It's Jack, with Jess and Sarah. They're right beside me, shouting, like they think that I can win. Win? Some power inside me surges. The village girl drops back, as though she's standing still.

Pa's by the tents, smoking with the men. Not watching. Stirring trouble, I can tell that much from here.

I look back at the track. Pine trees to my right, orange needles stabbing at my toes. I don't feel them. I'm running like there's a spring inside, that's been coiled back; released, so I'm flung forward, so fast that I can't stop.

The village ladies, they're doing their slow clap. The clap that says: "Well done, children," and, "Praise God we've done our duty, and dear Lorrie's going to win".

Perhaps she is, but that won't stop me from trying. I'm running for the deer and rabbits, for the adders that streak across the heaths and the slow-worms that curl beneath our tent. I'm running for Jack. For Ma. For Mr. Milner. Not Pa, though: I ain't done that for years.

The girl ahead, she's slowing. That, or I've speeded up. Faces lift. A hush. Old gals put down their knitting. Only Pa's got his head down, kicking at the dust.

A few more paces and I'm at her shoulder. She starts like she's frightened; like she didn't think I could be there.

In a moment I go past. Mouths hang open, like they've forgotten what to say. Then the shouting starts: "Lorr-ie!"

Her strides grow wider still. She's a motor-car that roars off up an empty road; a horse, set loose from its tethers; a dog that's seen a rabbit, too far from its hole.

I'm running just behind her, faster than I've ever run before.

"Lorr-ie, Lorr-ie!"

There's an edge to their voices, like something's going wrong. We're the thieving gypsies. We aren't meant to win.

Where's Mr. Milner? I pick out his straw hat, bobbing in the crowd. I strain to hear his voice. It isn't there. I turn my head towards him. He's smiling; smiling, like he's had the best news in the world.

I'm the stag that sprints off from the field edge, when Pa comes with his gun. The swift that skims the corn-field. Swooping, dipping, twisting: running for my life.

My toe strikes stone. A rock, that wasn't there last time I passed, that's meant to bring me down.

Pain shrieks. The nail hangs, half ripped off.

I can't put my foot down. I'm going to have to stop.

"Magg-ie!"

It's Jack's voice. Somehow he's beside me, pushing through the crowd.

"Don't stop, Maggie! Run!"

His face is scrunched, like he's trying not to cry. Jack hasn't stopped, I think. I've seen him laid out on his death-bed, like he'll never rise again. Each time, he snatches for more air. Each time, when Pa's already drinking off his sorrows, Jack holds Ma's hand and won't give in.

I run. A hundred yards to go.

Lorrie, from the ooh-ing and the aah-ing, she must know that I've been hurt. She's slowed, a victor's trot, waving to the crowd. My toe grinds, blood mixing with the dust. I'm used to being hurt. Keep going. I won't feel it 'til I stop.

Muscles clench in her firm calves. I see the pattern on her shoes, rippled, like a stream.

I go quietly, keeping my breath in. She's a rabbit that I'm stalking, that's forgotten that I'm there. The crowd cries out in warning. Her heels kick up once more.

I'm the horse Pa saw win the Derby up at Epsom. A bicycle, free-wheeling down Pitch Hill. An aeroplane, wings spread, silver in the sun.

Suddenly Ma's here beside me, knees up, skirts flouncing, bloomers on display. I've never seen her move so fast. Never knew that she could run.

Sarah, Jack, the gypsy kids – they're here from nowhere, yelling. Ladies, long necks craning. Mr. Milner at the finish: that big smile across his face.

And Pa? Pa's coming down the field towards me. "Come on, Maggie, lass," he shouts.

Inch by inch I'm making ground. I see the pale frizz on Lorrie's neck, the freckles on her arm.

Then she's behind me. The finish tape is moving, like it's getting closer by itself.

I'm going to do it. I'm going to shake Lorrie Chandler's hand and say: "Well run. Bad luck. I'm sure you'll beat me next time."

I'm the girl who will be gracious. I'm the girl who'll make Ma proud.

I'm the girl who'll reach the end and discover it's the start.

SOMETHING YOU NEED TO KNOW

"Look, Mum – an egg!"

Our daughter Maya points to something curved, just visible in the sand. Ingrid, our guide, scoops the pale form up and holds it out towards us: crumpled like a ping-pong ball, stepped on by mistake.

"Safely hatched," she says, and sets the empty turtle shell to rest on the damp sand.

Dawn light streaks Maya's shoulders as she crouches, watchful and intent. Early on an August morning, on a beach close to Greece's southern tip, we've come to search for sea turtles: to find how many of this threatened species have hatched out overnight.

With deft movements, Ingrid and two other conservation guides scoop away the sand. Most eggshells that emerge are curled and empty. Only a few come out intact, like small pink-fir potatoes. Knowing them too old to hatch, Ingrid breaks an egg apart: "This one stopped growing long ago."

I stare at the withered form inside: thinking of other tiny beings, barely formed, that lost the fight for life.

Not wishing to see, I glance at Maya's face. Will our tender-hearted daughter, not yet nine, grieve for this small creature? Turning, she slips her hand in mine. "Don't worry, Mum. It's nature's way. Not every baby turtle gets to live."

Where does this wisdom come from, far beyond her years? Her empathy and love for every living thing?

We stand, waves breaking at our toes, before the sweep

15

of Kalamata Bay. Small yachts dot the cove, bows pointing to the wind. A Greek flag flutters on the headland, proud.

We'd learnt about the sea turtles just the night before. Behind the bright-lit restaurants at the harbour, a shack stands in the shadows. Our daughter tugs us to see the photographs of sea turtles, *Caretta caretta*, pinned up on its doors. "This year, we have a hundred nests along our shore," a young woman in a T-shirt tells us. "Twenty years ago, that number was just forty." If we pay a little money, we can adopt a sea turtle ourselves.

Our daughter's gold-flecked eyes light up.

"Please Mum, can we adopt one? Can we, Dad?"

Her father Tim and I exchange a glance. I guess that, like me, he thinks of the wild creatures already taken to her heart. Rhino, puffin, polar bear, short-eared owl, brown-hairstreak butterfly, a rare and special newt: all we have paid a small sum to 'adopt'. Their pictures fill her bedroom walls; certificates in frames confirming the species she supports. All bring a new soft-toy, to be cradled to her chest each night.

"Oh Maya," I say. "Don't you have enough already?"

"Please –"

How can we deny her when every creature needs our help? When her yearning gaze implores us?

I think of nights stood at our daughter's door, listening for the soft rush of her breath.

A form is quickly filled, a credit card passed over. Next morning, young conservation volunteers – two Germans and a Greek – will check the beach for nests.

So it is that, next day, our family of three is up before the dawn.

The sun, inching higher, strikes the distant, tree-cloaked mountains. Beside the beach, orange-pink roofs of tourist villas show through the bamboo groves. In spring, female turtles come up from the sea at night, to lay their eggs amid the sun-loungers and palm-leaf fringed umbrellas. Man and nature, existing side by side.

Maya runs ahead. I hear her voice rise, sharp.

Sea turtle eggs — three dozen or more — lie smashed. The tracks of animals — foxes, dogs, perhaps a cat or two — mill round them. Our guides draw in their breath and drop down to the still-damp sand.

Painstakingly, they count the broken shells. Thirty-seven eggs, dug up and feasted on. Streaks of golden yolk glint in the morning sun.

Among the scattered shells, a thin dark form lies still. Its limbs, dusted with pale sand, are stiff. A turtle that will never swim amid the cresting waves or hunt around the rocks.

Tim hides it with his body, so Maya will not see.

She's looking the other way, at something on the sand.

"Come here," she calls.

From the half-broken shell beside her, a small black flipper waves.

"Alive," the whisper of excitement passes round.

Ingrid crouches. "We must leave it. Tonight, this one will have another chance."

Our guides return the survivor to its nest, then gently press the sand. On top, they add a metal grid, stabbed through with bamboo canes. As last defence, a printed notice: "Please DO NOT DISTURB. *Caretta caretta* is protected by Law."

"Animals can't read," Maya says, as our little group, subdued, moves on. "It's not the dogs' and foxes' fault. They get hungry too."

That same warm understanding, for every living thing. I think of our daughter's narrow bed back home, submerged beneath a sea of small soft-toys. Each one, a keepsake of a species she's adopted; each to be caressed and comforted before she goes to sleep.

"It's almost like she knows," I said to Tim one night, back home, lying wakeful at his side.

"How can she know?" His voice came gruff with sleep.

"She does. I know she does. It's almost like – with all her endless animals – she's doing it to hurt us."

"No, Linz. Not Maya." My husband pushed up on one elbow. "Our girl would never hurt us. She'd never hurt a fly."

It wasn't hard, our decision not to tell her. We made it on the day we brought her home. February 22nd, 2015: the day we got the papers and this longed-for child became our own. The date we mark each year, unspoken: watching as she tends her precious toys.

Why tell her when the truth would hurt her, and ruin the life we've made?

The sun grows hotter, beating on our heads.

Our daughter skips away in front. Beside her, a volley ball court is marked out on the sand. What if a turtle makes her nest beneath it? What if the players' pounding feet destroy the buried eggs within?

"Mum? Dad?" Maya's face blazes like a sunbeam. "Look over here!"

We hurry to her side. Beside her are a maze of tiny markings: like tracks of minute tractors, circling, then heading to the sea.

Our guides' gazes soften. They kneel and point, showing where each set of tracks reaches to the waves.

I seek my husband's eye; finding my own joy, reflected.

Ingrid traces with her finger the tangled whorl of tracks. "Seventeen came to the sea. Maybe more will hatch, tonight."

"Mum! Dad!" our daughter calls.

A grey shape lies beside her on the sand. Its small limbs twitch. A hatchling, still alive.

Eager bodies crowd. We form a wall, to shield it from the sun.

The turtle's flailing flippers brush against the sand.

"For Maya," I will this stranded creature. "For Maya, make it to the sea."

Instead, the hatchling seems to lose its way. It turns, and crawls back up the beach.

"Do not touch," Ingrid commands, as hands reach out to help. "We must let it find its way."

Tim's fingers link with mine.

We stand and watch, as nature takes its course. In the distance, children splash and squeal.

I stare out at the bay.

When I look again, the fragile form has changed direction. Seeming to find its bearings, it heads towards the sea.

Gulls soar above. We hide the toiling creature from their eyes and claws.

As though it knows its home is near, the turtle's speed increases. One last brave push and — gathered by a wave — the hatchling is afloat. For an instant, its body seems to hang, unmoving. Then, legs and flippers whirring, it dives into the depths.

Our daughter wades into the water, straining to see it go.

My husband's fingers tighten, as though to tell me: yes.

Never, we said back home. Never would we tell her and lose the happiness we have.

Now, as new life quickens in a warm Greek sea, we take our daughter's hands.

"Maya," I say. "Your Dad and I, we love you. There's something you need to know."

FIGHT OR FLIGHT, APRIL 1916

"Meet me at the fountain, 2pm."

Your pencilled note faded off to nothing. I'd know which one you meant.

I got there first, of course. Your kind of fountain, I thought as I arrived: three muscled horses cast in bronze, hooves clashing high above. Atop, the Duke of Somewhere, brandishing his sword.

I waited, as the hands slipped round the clock. I was used to your dashed instructions – 'refreshment room at Crewe', 'southbound platform, 5.04'. In those days you were on the move: to Manchester on Battalion business, Aldershot for a court martial, then off to some windswept Midlands camp where your toes froze in your socks. Barking orders, losing what was left of your thin hair. Still in England: still champing to get out.

Two thirty came and went. Other girls were waiting, peeking at their watches, just like me. Trying to ignore the tide of men in khaki, with their hungry, blatant stares.

Two forty-five. Had I come to the wrong fountain? Perhaps there was another, scarcely different, on the far side of the Barracks. The army likes its symmetry, after all. If I went to look, I might find you there, tutting and impatient. *Stay where you are, Bea,* I told myself. *Don't take a risk. Edward won't be happy if you're late.*

Two pigeons were parading by the fountain. To pass the time, I watched them: a charcoal male, plumped-up chest thrust out, waddling in pursuit of a smaller, sleeker female. If he fell back, to peck a fallen crumb, this female bird peered back. Come on, keep up, her pert gaze seemed to say. *Who led on who*, I thought?

At five to three, I made myself a bargain. If you had not arrived before the pigeons flew away, I too would be off, heading back to Bruton Street. The accounts girls would have the kettle warm, to read the tale of my blotched cheeks and pour me cups of tea.

"Bea – the Adjutant asked to see me, I couldn't get away –"

You, in your officer's uniform, boots bright as new-hatched conkers. Eyebrows knitting upwards in that way that made my heart spin like a coin.

I tried my hardest to look stern.

"You're not angry, Bea? Don't be fierce. I came the instant that I could." One corner of your mouth curved up. "They need me back in just an hour. Why don't we go to a hotel?"

The other waiting girls were looking on, smiles slipping down their faces. Your finger on my forehead eased away my frown. "The Autumn Days are over, aren't they, Bea?"

"Just about." My monthly bleed went on so long, I never knew for sure.

You kissed my hand as though I were a duchess; for all those girls to see.

"Come on then, Bea, why are we waiting? Let's do it, while we can."

Afterwards, as we lay on that hard, damp-smelling bed, you rose above me, head propped on one arm. Your face was half

22

in shadow.

"I'm going out."

"Out?" I was sat up in an instant, palms sliding on the thin brown counterpane.

You touched my cheek. "Don't look so surprised. We've been expecting it, haven't we?"

We had, of course we had.

"When?"

Your hand, scented of our passion and tobacco, stroked my face.

"Three days, they say. I'll have time to pop down to Dad and Mother. Tell Ethel, up in Scotland, if I can –"

By then I wasn't listening. I was floundering, not-waving-but-drowning, in your brown, fall-into-me eyes. We knew each other pretty well, by then. For almost two years we'd been meeting in hotel rooms on the wrong side of the tracks. Sharing our private moments with mice that scuttled in the wainscot and bugs that nipped inside the sheets. Not that I had minded. For two years we'd been king and queen of everything, wrapped in one another's arms.

"Remember what we said, Bea? That our time was short, how short we couldn't know, so we'd jolly well make the most of it. And we've done that, little girl, haven't we, the very best way that we can?"

I thought of the long, dark lists of names that filled the newspapers each day. Died of wounds. Missing in action. Odd turns of phrase, made commonplace.

Often, when we met, you'd bring along *The Times*. Sit with your pipe, when your desire for me was done, and scan those brutal lists. Sometimes you'd look up, empty-faced, and tell me, that a friend of yours was gone. Other times you

23

were silent, and I'd know it, just the same.

"Where will you go?"

"France, to start."

The wooden bedhead dug into my spine. The small, dim room was fogged. I thought what I'd be doing if I hadn't got your note. Out with Bessie, maybe, my best friend from accounts. Out on Oxford Street, buying your favourite coal tar soap and an ounce of macaroons. Careless, carefree things I wouldn't do again.

"Why didn't you tell me?"

"I've only just heard myself. I wrote the minute that I could. I'm sorry we won't have time to see a show. Go somewhere grand for dinner, the way we always planned –"

"You mean – after this – I won't see you?"

You swung round to kneel astride me, pushing up my dress. "What – leave my little girl, so sad and lonely?" Your lips bowed down to mine, your index finger running up my thigh. I pulled away, looking for the rubbers you made sure we always used.

"Come on, Bea." Bunching the fabric of my dress, you kissed the soft skin of my stomach. "In three days I'll be fighting for my country. It's your patriotic duty, to give me what I need."

OCTOBER 1917, CARLTON VALE NW6

Two weeks since your last letter. Some days, I push the pram up to the reading room and scan the long, grey lists. They don't like babies there: not ones like ours, who scowls and bangs his fists. Just like his father, I want to say, to tease you; to see your fall-into-me eyes light up again.

He's crying now, as usual. After so many months, you'd think I'd have the wit to read his cries. That angry bawl? *'I'm hungry.'* That piercing yell? *'My napkin's full, again.'* For me, it's not so simple. What messages our baby sends pass above my head. Instead, I sit beside the window and watch the pigeons on the roof.

My sister wrote to let you know about the boy. She said you had the right to know. I kicked and screamed when I found out: telling her I hated her, just like I hated you. Perhaps her letter pricked your conscience. You've paid for this room for us to live in. Aren't I the lucky one?

The thunder of the guns. We hear it sometimes, even here. How long in such an onslaught can one man stay alive?

Each letter brings you closer, then pushes you away. A few short, pencilled phrases: *'safe behind lines'*; *'my love to you and the dear boy.'* Each month you send us money, to a bank that's far away. I took two buses, once, to fetch it, the boy quiet in his pram. The manager shook his jowls at us, reproving. I won't go there again.

Your letters tell me little: only that, at the moment that you wrote them, you were still alive. What has happened in the long days since, as your letter weaved its way from France? Are you behind lines still, with a fresh-laid egg for breakfast? Or drowned in a shell-hole, like so many men you knew.

Me? I'm not alive: not in the way I was before. Not in the eyes of people who once loved me. Strumpet: that's what my Father told me, on the day he threw me out. That's what the ladies of the church think as they peer into the pram.

Sometimes, when the guns are quiet, you write us longer letters. You tell me what you dream of: our boy growing up, not in London, but in the country: strong and free, his limbs browned by the sun. The three of us, in a pretty, whitewashed cottage, with roses round the door.

In the nine months while my body swelled, you became a hero. 2nd Lieutenant Edward Ede, the day you left, so proud of your commission. Soon promoted to Lieutenant, then to Captain; twice mentioned in Despatches. Awarded a fine medal for your courage under fire. Acting Major, you wrote in your last letter – 'imagine that, Bea, your Edey! A big thing's coming, Bea. Be ready. Be strong, whatever happens, for our boy.'

The baby's cries are getting louder. Before I go to him, I heave the window up and shout out to the birds. "Be off," I tell the puffed-up male pigeon, and flap my hands until he lurches into flight. Fly away, I beg the slight, coquettish female at his side. Spread your wings, little girl. Take flight, while still you have the chance.

BECOMING YOUR BEST YOU

"Take a seat," said the girl in the white coat.

Jenny lowered herself on to the silver disc of metal, supported by a slender pedestal. It wobbled at her weight. She imagined the thin stool buckling, tipping her to the floor.

"I won't keep you a moment."

The make-up girl's skin appeared unnatural, as though painted with a roller. Thick black lashes ringed her eyes. Jenny thought of the crumpled legs of house spiders, that came to her lounge carpet to die.

Inching her hands down, she grasped the twisted plastic handles of her shopping. She did not have to stay. While the girl was not looking, she could slip down from the stool, push past the ranks of sharp-edged, gilded boxes with their scientific French, past the young men squirting perfume, and out into the safety of the street—

"Mrs Hartley?"

Warmth flowed to Jenny's face as she released the handles of the bags.

"It is hot, isn't it?" The girl fanned her honey-coloured neck with a clipboard. "I'm Tara, by the way."

If Tara sensed Jenny's longing for escape, her lilting voice did not betray it. Were make-up girls like vicars: specially trained, to treat all-comers the same?

"Please – call me Jenny."

Re-perching on the stool, Jenny confronted her reflection in the mirror. In the unforgiving lights, her cheeks hung down like curtains, pooling round her jaw. Her nose, inherited from her father, was ruddy at the tip. Beneath, her mouth, chin and neck merged together, as though giving up the fight for separate life. What foolishness had made her think a make-up session titled 'Becoming Your Best You' might cheer her up?

"Have you come for something special?" the girl, Tara, asked, tilting her sleek head.

"Not particularly." Although her choice to be here was, in its way, remarkable: a throwback to her younger, bolder self. Not since her teens had Jenny entrusted her appearance to another's hands. What would Peter say, if he knew that she had come?

"Got a party coming up? Or a wedding?"

"Not really —"

"You just felt ready for a change?"

In the mirror, the girl's spidery eyes roved over Jenny's face.

"Not exactly. It's just that — I suppose I'm here really — well, I've come because I'm sad."

The truth, let out by mistake, spread through the fragrant air between them: a discharge, discolouring a river.

"I'm sorry to hear that." The girl fiddled with some little pots beside her.

"Don't be," Jenny covered. "I'm talking nonsense, that is all."

"Are you wearing any make-up?" the girl asked, in a brisker tone.

"None at all."

This Jenny could answer happily, for decades had passed since she last bothered with the stuff. Peter used to say he liked her as she was.

"I'll just give your face a little clean —"

The girl leaned closer — as though her white coat, like a doctor's, gave unfettered access to Jenny's personal space — and wiped something cold and moist across her forehead. Slip, slap. Jenny's mother had mopped her face in just such a quick, efficient way, if custard had dribbled down her chin.

"Now, for your skin — we'll start with some concealer —" Tara appraised the colours on the tray beside her with the air of an Old Master.

If any skin should be concealed, it was Jenny's own: rosaceous on her cheeks, age-spotted round her hair-line. Most mornings, she glimpsed fresh lines on her sixty-something face: intruders, that snuck in as she slept.

Tara's finger, daubed with beige, appeared before her nose. "How does this look, Jenny?"

"Oh, just put it on."

Perhaps her tone was terser than she meant, for the make-up girl was quiet, dotting pale fluid, then whisking back and forwards with a brush, burrowing into crevices. A brush, for goodness' sake — delicate as an artist's — for what, in Jenny's day, was still known as foundation? She wondered how long Tara must spend, perfecting her painted face for work. Was that what the dungaree-clad women of her generation had fought for: that young women should have the right — Jenny saw them each week on the bus — to resemble plastic dolls?

Still, she should not judge. Who knew what brought Tara to this line of work? Perhaps she was paying her way through university. Perhaps — the thought came with a pang — she was a would-be actress, between jobs, swapping greasepaint for the subtler shades of Estée Lauder. A person not so different, after all, from the girl Jenny once had been herself.

Hard to believe now, Jenny thought, as Tara blotted more concealer on the inner corners of her eyes, how fiercely she had longed to leave suburban Jenny Brookes behind and take her chances on the stage! A character actress, perhaps, for she had seemed to have a gift for comedy. A dream that she had clung to for years; until it proved impossible, with a family like hers.

She remembered the evening long ago, when her parents, in hats and tightly buttoned coats, arrived to watch her school production. Jenny's part was small: a Roman servant girl. Her main task was to walk on stage and kneel beside her dying elder sister, without an explosive cracking of her knees.

Afterwards, in the school hall, proud families reunited with their daughters. As she rushed up to her parents' side, her mother took one look and turned away. "Nothing better than – a French tart," her father exclaimed, so loudly that the whole room was struck silent. And although Jenny had only a hazy idea of what a French tart might involve, she knew it to be more than pastry and strawberry jam.

At home, when the offending colours on her face had been removed, her mother addressed her gravely. "You will need to be careful, Jenny, when you are older. Not to look – well, you know –" Though her mother lacked the vocabulary to explain exactly what she meant, Jenny grasped her meaning nonetheless. And, though her make-up had been put on by a teacher, and so was not her fault, she felt guilty and somehow dirtied, knowing her parents thought less of her as a result.

"So – what's left you feeling sad?" the make-up girl was saying now, nuzzling her brush into the open pores round Jenny's nose.

And – as though this close proximity of their bodies compelled her, again, to answer honestly – Jenny said: "Because someone I love has died."

"Oh." The brushing stopped. "I'm sorry."

"Don't be." Jenny smiled, as though her dear friend Carl's dreadful death really did not matter. "It's too late now. Nothing can be done."

The girl's shining eyes, meeting hers in the mirror, seemed to overflow with sympathy; and it struck Jenny that, of anyone in the world, only Tara knew that she was sad.

Even to herself, she had barely voiced this fact. Her affection for Carl had grown imperceptibly, over many years. Only when disease spread remorseless through his body, and she lay at night beside her husband, her nightie and the top edge of the duvet soaked with silent tears, had she found out that she loved him.

They had met at an amateur dramatics group, early in her marriage. After a few years, during which her roles had grown in size, Peter asked her to stop going. He did not like men looking at her on the stage. Without protest, she withdrew from the group. Instead, she began to help in other ways, selling programmes or helping out with scenery and props. In this way, she still saw Carl, who was often present, overseeing things backstage. During rehearsals, they would sit on the strip of grass behind the hall and eat their sandwiches. Talking, always talking. Although with other people, even Peter, she found little to say.

And now, three decades on, dear Carl was dead. A man who was not her partner, husband, boyfriend, lover, father, son, nor any other handy label she could grasp to pin on to her grief. Carl had merely been a man she saw now and then, in whose company she had unfurled like a rose.

Something wet rolled down her cheek.

"Thank you," Jenny whispered, as Tara pressed a tissue to her hand. "Quite all right," she added, dabbing at her eyes. "Sorry to be silly."

The girl leant over her with a waft of floral perfume. "Eyes closed now, if you don't mind."

Eye shadow. Something else her father had not liked, along with lipstick, nail varnish, shortened skirts, high heels, shiny knee boots and anything else that drew attention to the female form. Jenny held her breath as Tara pressed a soft stick deep into the creases of her eye, then smoothed a creamy paste across the lid.

"I'm sad too," the girl said, as she blended the colours in.

"Are you?"

Jenny's eyes flicked open. Tara had turned away, mixing something on her small white plastic tray.

"Why are you sad?" Jenny asked. It had not occurred to her that such a flawless person might be unhappy.

"My flatmate isn't well."

"I'm sorry to hear that."

The girl swept a lighter colour over Jenny's brow. "She's in hospital right now." Her breath came light and quick. "She's got — you know, what that woman had on the telly. The one who dressed up as a — you know — "

Surprisingly, for she watched little television, Jenny knew exactly. The woman, too young and beautiful to die — who spoke up about her unspeakable disease — had been ill around the same time as Carl.

"I'm sorry," she said again. "Maybe you can go to see your friend, after work?"

The girl shook her head. "Too much risk of infection. She's having radiation."

"It's amazing what they can do, these days," Jenny said, though the doctors had found little to help Carl.

"They've told her to expect the worst."

"Oh — that's hard to bear —"

Jenny pictured the young woman, dying, whose cheerful face had filled the news bulletins. Who, to raise awareness of her embarrassing type of cancer, had sat in TV studios dressed up as a — what? Jenny could barely bring herself to think the word.

After the incident at the play, when her father had shouted 'French tart' in front of everyone, she had gone home and washed her hands. In the space of a few days, this urge to wash her hands became her life. Barely had she scrubbed them clean than her hands felt dirty, and she had to start again. Her skin dried out, her knuckles split and bled.

Her school asked her to stay at home, lest her 'contagion' spread. She stayed in her bedroom which, handily, was right beside the bathroom. "Pull yourself together," her father snapped, if their paths crossed on the landing.

The make-up girl, Tara, gave a sniff. "It's not like we're best friends or anything. I haven't even known her very long. The thing is, she's my flatmate, but she's gone back to her parents. Without her, I can't pay the rent. The landlord's given me notice. I've got to leave in three days' time."

"Have you got somewhere to go?"

"The landlord's keeping our deposit. I can't get another place without one. Anyway –" The girl sighed, then handed Jenny a round mirror. "Tell me what you think so far."

"Good Lord. Is that me?"

Her eyes were twice as large, and somehow had changed colour, from their usual blueish grey to startling cobalt. Her lips were full and pink, her mouth, chin and neck entirely separate.

"Tart," came her father's voice, from nowhere.

"Happy so far?"

"Yes – thank you –" Despite her father, Jenny's spirits lifted by a notch. "But what will you do, in that case? About finding somewhere else to live?"

It was not her place to ask, Jenny knew. Yet, in talking about Carl, some tight-wound part of her had loosened.

"I don't know. I've got to stick around, for my job. It's harder to rent when you're alone."

Jenny thought of her son's old bedroom that she had cleared the month before, in hope it might give shelter to a family from Ukraine. For two weeks she had scrubbed and dusted, bringing in new furniture and knick-knacks, picturing the people who might live there.

But Peter had said no. Their house had just one bathroom. He did not wish to share it with people he did not know.

They would get to know whoever came, Jenny had pointed out. Their guests would soon become their friends.

But Peter had put his foot down; in the same way her father did, when she was young.

34

And alongside Peter and her father, she thought of other men. Men who, after she had at last got over her compulsion to wash her hands, had leant out of their car as they drove by. Whistling, they cupped their hands against their chests, in reference to her own substantial breasts, which swayed in her cheesecloth top as she walked. After which, she had thrown the top into the bin, along with many others; and swathed herself instead in fuller clothes and steel-wired bras like missile heads.

When she looked up, Tara was holding a thin pencil. She began to flick it, in deft, scratchy movements, through Jenny's left eyebrow. Jenny saw that, over the years, without her really noticing, her brows had lost their colour. The one on the right was the hue of old knickers, put too often through the wash. Whereas the brow on the left, thanks to Tara, was emerging in a graceful, mid-brown arc.

"You try."

Tara held the pencil out towards her.

"Take that rubbish off!" her father shouted in her head.

"I can't —"

"It's easy. Watch, I'll show you again."

With a hand that trembled only slightly, Jenny copied Tara's tiny, upward marks, until the right brow roughly matched the left. A new, enlivened version of her face stared back.

"You know, Tara — we have a room at home that isn't used," this new, enlivened face began to say. "It's really nothing special. But you'd be welcome to stay there, if it helped —"

The girl seemed to go still.

35

"You could come and look at it, to see if it would suit you. There's just me and Peter, my husband, left at home. You could stay as long you needed. No rent to pay, of course —"

She thought of the brave woman on the news, in her brown, curved costume, her smiling face poking from the top. Somehow, she had found the strength to make the very best of her sad situation: warning about symptoms, so others could avoid her plight. And Carl too had made peace with the fact that he was dying, and put his affairs in order and reached out to his children, who lived around the globe. Close to the end, his thin, bruised hand had reached for hers. "I love you, Jenny," he had said. While she, who loved him back, had stared mutely at the floor, unable to reply because of Peter.

"Turd," she said suddenly, picturing not the woman from TV, but Peter, dressed up like a smelly brown banana.

"Sorry?"

Jenny twisted, to look into Tara's puzzled face. "Come and live with us and see how you get on. Until you've got some money saved. Until you get back on your feet."

She imagined going home and telling Peter — in a voice that brooked no argument — that she had met a young woman in need of a home. For too long, her own life had been defined by small disasters. This very weekend, Tara would come to live with them. She would stay, and use their bathroom, for however long she liked.

INCIDENT ON THE LINE

Her phone rings at the moment the tube train breaks off from its moorings up the track. The string of silver carriages sways towards her, the driver growing visible, chin propped on his hands.

"I don't know quite how to say this," a voice comes in Katja's ear. "But would you like some eggs?"

Eggs? She thinks of brown eggs in their box, flicking the soft lid open as she does each Saturday in the supermarket queue, to check they are not cracked. Quails' eggs: smaller, greenish, speckled. Barn eggs, farm eggs, free-range, organic, eggs with added vitamins, eggs with Omega—

"Hello?"

"I'm here," Katja says.

The tube doors part, passengers disgorging, manoeuvring their hard-edged suitcases down on to the platform.

A ripple passes through the men and women standing by: a synaptic firing that will carry them on through the deepest confines of the Piccadilly line, up escalators, through thrumming streets and coffee shops, on to the sanctuary of their offices and wide, grey, empty desks.

She does not follow them. Instead, relinquishing her place, she sits down on a bench.

Ruth, whose voice comes down the line, has never phoned her. Her tone is half embarrassed: as though Katja may ask her to call back later on.

"How are you?" Katja says, as her mind rattles through the reasons for this call. Ruth is the sister of Evie, her oldest friend. Is Evie ill? Unlikely, Katja thinks, for Ruth's voice seems nervous, not alarmed. Did she imagine that, at the start, Ruth mentioned eggs?

Hope – familiar, foolish – seeps into her veins. She beats it back. Hope is not her friend. Hope is what she feels when doctors peer into her notes, and needles pierce her skin, and her hormones flow and ebb, and she and Cal, her husband, wait, through weeks and months and years, for a thing that does not happen.

"Evie told me what's been going on."

Evie, to whom, two days ago, Katja confided the unseemly rollercoaster ride of her struggle to conceive. A truth she now regrets confessing, for how has poor Evie felt, to have such misery flung over her? Bitter, fetid words, that carry, beneath their stench, a whisper: why me? Why me, not you? Why do you have three children, while I have none?

Another train is peeling up the track. Katja sits, hunched over her phone: saying, by her posture, do not come near. Do not ask if I will move my bag so you may sit down.

And perhaps her fellow commuters – attuned as they are to each others' bodies and the distance, finely calibrated, that must be kept between them – read her signal, for not one of them approaches.

And Ruth is saying, in a cheerful tone: "I have two boys now, I'm not planning any more." And: "So I'm wondering whether you would like – whether I could give you – some of my eggs?"

And with those words, heard for a second time, so Katja cannot be mistaken, a tsunami bursts inside her. Her life is overturned, her body sucked into the surf, spun and tumbled, spat out, abandoned and regathered, like a sand grain on a beach.

As she wheels and pitches, thoughts rush to her head. Ruth is younger: four years younger, she remembers, from the days when she and Evie played together, and Ruth was the little sister, imposing on their games. Thirty-four, Ruth must be now; compared to the thirty-eight that Katja is herself.

What a difference those four years make, to the men and women who inhabit the clinics she now frequents. To them, she has discovered, thirty-four means possibility. While thirty-eight means eggs that – "forgive me, Mrs – uh – Chalke –" have passed their use-by date.

She stares at the dark-stained constellations, left by chewing gum, that dot the platform edge. The tracks, weeds, caressing couples round her, fade. There is only her voracious longing, and the voice at the far end of the line.

"Thank you," Katja says, over and over. At some point she stands up and drops her leather glove. Not until the evening will she find the glove is missing. Since it is new – a present from Cal, who endures this with her – she will try hard to track it down. Even at the lost property office at Baker Street she will not find it: so the glove, in her mind, becomes a sacrificial object, that must be lost, to enable whatever happens next.

"You are sure?" she says.

The crucial question, etched already in her heart: for how can Ruth, who does not know her well, be willing to undergo whatever medical procedures are required? Some of which she has experienced herself, and knows to be invasive and unpleasant?

And Ruth is reassuring, overflowing with kindness and conviction; asking what she should do next.

"I'll find out," Katja says.

She thinks of the little room, where an Italian doctor has informed her that donated eggs are what she needs. A suggestion that, for all his charmingly-accented English, has seemed impossible; for whom could she ask for such a thing, when she has no sister, and her closest friends are the age she is herself, and thus – in the plain talk of the clinics – over the hill?

Hearing this, the doctor has hinted at an international marketplace – an ova pick-n-mix, as she imagines it – where eggs may be bought and sold. And Katja, knowing by instinct that such a place, while it may offer hope, is not for her, has felt her dream diminish.

And now, on a suburban station where she has stood a thousand times, an offer has blown in on the breeze.

Then the call is over.

Besuited men and women are trickling down the steps, the next train trundling down the track: familiar sights she cannot comprehend.

In the years she has spent trying to conceive, a wind has blown against her.

Katja does not know, as she boards the train and surges into Northfields, that, with Ruth, that wind will change direction.

She does not know, as the train slips into South Ealing, that she will say many times in the months ahead: "Are you sure?" And: "Don't feel you can't change your mind." For she understands the burden of her hope, and does not want Ruth to bend beneath it too.

She does not know, as the train enters Acton Town, that Ruth will say, "Don't worry. I want this to work, as much as you do." Or that Ruth's eggs, under a microscope, will gleam with youth and health.

She does not know, as the train sinks underground, that, when two small embryos are implanted, each one will seize the chance to grow. Or that, on the morning she takes a pregnancy test – as a huge gas explosion rocks her part of London – the line will show up blue.

She does not know, as the train nudges into Gloucester Road, that two babies will be born: too early and too small, in anxious, frightened days. Or that those tiny, wrinkled forms will grow up strong and true.

She does not know, as the doors slam open at Green Park, that each boy will one day say to her: "You are not my mother". Words she will hear and weather, for to say them is their right; and motherhood is a bucking horse, that sometimes throws her off.

How can she know, as she ascends on a silver staircase to the street, that her sons and Ruth's will form their own connections? That, from this confluence of science and human kindness, a tube-map of relationships will flow? Or that, in the time it takes to reach her wide, grey desk – or so it feels – two young men, grown, will head off up the tracks?

TIDE CHANGE AT THE
NO-EYE-CONTACT CAFE

From all four walls, creatures seemed to swoop towards them: swans, beating their strong wings, geese with necks out-stretched, warblers flitting from the reeds. In the flooded fields behind, water shone in silver threads. Amidst it all, Simon stood in his black T-shirt, camera slung around his neck, muscles in his forearms lightly flexing. He had no idea, Cate understood, of how she might reply.

She hadn't wanted 'regulars' when she'd opened up the Boatyard Café. Indeed, she'd set out to discourage them. She did not want to be the kind of café owner who invited confidences. Her aim was to be anonymous: to pass from her cottage opposite to drop off a fresh-baked carrot cake or marmalade sponge; to check used mugs were left, as instructed, in the dishwasher; and then to slip back home. Did people wonder, as they stopped off at the small, DIY café, halfway between the village and the National Trust house on the hill, who supplied the cakes and Arabica coffee? Let them wonder, Cate thought. So long as they left a few coins in payment, and wiped up any spills, she was content.

The No-Eye-Contact Café, her brother Will called it. He was mocking her, she knew, and yet – as only siblings could – Will had hit the nail on the head. He was out there in the boatyard now, patching some old hulk. Her brother, who once built software for a big Swiss bank; but now preferred, as she did, to live beside the river Tamar, the edges of their old lives softened by its changing tides.

She'd been glad of Will's decision, after Adam died; and the boatyard, with its aged, peeling craft, became her responsibility. She'd never thought, when she and Adam took on the place together, that five years on she'd be a widow, trying to run the boatyard on her own. How relieved she'd been, when Will stepped in to help.

It was thanks to her brother that the Boatyard Café had come about. Some mornings, she'd make a cake, to have with their coffee. If any was left, she'd put it in the boatyard kitchen, with a sign inviting walkers to come in and help themselves.

Passers-by, Will reported, enjoyed the cake but wanted tea and coffee too. Cate had plenty of old mugs and plates she never used. The boatyard kitchen, small and dingy, had a sink, a fridge and a yellowed dishwasher in one corner. She swept away the cobwebs, bought tea-pots in a charity shop and new, silver cafetieres. The little room beside the kitchen had two old brown leather sofas and an eccentric, worn-out Louis IV-style chair. They would do, Cate thought. Most likely no customers would come at all. If they did, they could sit outside and watch the shifting tides.

Whatever people chose to do, she did not want to see them. Not with grief weighing her down, like a suit of chainmail armour. No, Cate thought: the café could run itself. She would oversee it from afar, spiriting in cakes and milk, for visitors to help themselves.

The village, on the Cornwall side of the river, had a forgotten feel. In the 19th century, its steep south-facing slopes had been mined for copper, tin and arsenic. After that, as mining gave way to market gardening, daffodils and strawberries were sent by train to London. Now, such industries were gone. Peace, or lethargy, had settled on the village. Change of any kind was usually opposed.

Yet, to Cate's surprise, people were stopping at the café. The cakes – coffee and walnut, almond and rosewater – placed under glass domes inherited from her mother, were greedily consumed. At weekends, three cakes were needed, sometimes even four.

Her customers seemed happy, for payments were left in the little wooden box. Her prices were lower than at the café in the village. The coins she scooped out every evening were enough to live on, for a simple existence was all that she required.

Though the villagers liked things to stay the same, change was coming nonetheless. Cate learnt of it from leaflets left on the sofa. A flood prevention scheme was being proposed. Water meadows, close to the village centre, were to be flooded. Instead of defences to hold the Tamar back, the river bank would be breached. Rare tidal wetlands would result.

"Write to your parish council," the leaflet urged. "Write to your MP! This madness must be stopped!"

One May evening, Cate went out to make her mind up for herself. The tide was low, ducks upending in the mud. Lady's smock, delicate mauve-pink flowers, danced along the path. She remembered walking this way with Adam. A small bird churred, clinging to a reed. "Stonechat," Adam might have said. Or perhaps, "sedge-warbler". It surprised her that, with Adam gone, river-bank life went on as before. She imagined the fields beside the path transformed into a wetland. How glad Adam would be, for the birds he loved to have a bigger, better home. Back at the café, she hid the leaflets out of sight.

Change proved irresistible, for a government quango was involved. A battle to keep the riverside path open was fought and won. After two years of discussion, the river bank was breached. A fine wooden bridge kept the footpath open and allowed the new wetlands to be viewed.

All this would have meant little to the No-Eye-Contact Café, had it not been for the birds. Within weeks, new species, snipe, teal, perhaps even an osprey, were sighted. Birders, in their many-pocketed waistcoats, were sighted too. And after them came Simon.

Cate hadn't noticed him at first. He was sitting, camouflaged by his black T-shirt against the dark brown sofa, editing his photographs.

"Hello," he said, as she passed through to the kitchen, in a low voice that almost made her drop her chocolate sponge.

"Oh – good afternoon," Cate answered. In the safety of the kitchen, she lifted the glass dome and pushed the cake inside. Someone – hopefully not the man on the sofa – had left their cup out of the dishwasher. She tidied it away. Then – for the only route out was through the room with the sofas – she swept past, gaze averted.

"Great cake," the man called behind.

He came several times after that. More than once she heard him talking to Will about some new lens he planned to buy. He – his name was Simon, Will told her – was a wildlife photographer. He was visiting the village to see which new species turned up at the wetlands. Bypassing the café in the village, he preferred to walk up to the boatyard.

He had a knack of sitting quietly, so Cate did not notice him. More often than she liked she strode into the café, thinking it was empty, to find him taking shelter from the

46

rain.

"Have you always been a photographer?" she asked once. With his tightly-cut T-shirt and fashionably-trimmed white beard, she thought he'd mention some trendy art school. Instead he said: "Post Office. Accountant. When they laid me off, I thought I'd follow my dream." He gestured to his camera, nestled like a cat upon his lap.

Cate smiled, pointing to her cottage, as though some urgent business – a cake, starting to tinge brown – awaited. "Well, I'll see you another day."

And see him she had, though not through her own choosing. It was extraordinary how often Simon – the timing of his visits determined by the tides – surprised her as she carried in a loaf-cake or replenished the Arabica coffee.

One day he showed her a photo of an otter: surfacing from the river, its whiskered face seeming to grin back in delight.

"Beautiful," Cate declared; forgetting, again, that she did not speak to customers.

And then, one day, like a migratory bird headed to new climes, Simon was gone.

She didn't miss him at first – or pretended she did not.

"Where's Simon?" she asked Will casually when two weeks had passed.

"Simon? He's in Alaska."

"Alaska?" Her stomach lurched.

"He said he'd email to let you know. He's on assignment, for a wildlife magazine."

How glamorous, Cate thought. How wonderful that their friend's career was taking off.

"He'll be back in a month," Will said.

He won't, Cate thought. Why would a photographer as sought-after as Simon return to a backwater like theirs?

To take her mind off what felt oddly like disappointment, she decided to spruce the café up. Takings were steady. She could afford to whitewash the walls, buy a blackboard for young children, set plants along the window.

She caught herself, more than once, thinking about Simon. How contented he had seemed, to sit upon her sofa. As though – or perhaps this was just her imagination – there was no other place he'd rather be. Silly, Cate told herself. She'd checked her emails and found that, sure enough, he'd written before he left. His name was Simon Clark. There were photographers everywhere named Simon Clark; too many to track him down.

And so her breath caught sharply when, one September morning, a man approached the boatyard, a bulky bag upon one shoulder, inhaling the river air. She stepped out from her kitchen.

"Cate?"

His skin was tanned and leathered, as though he'd spent long hours in wind and sun.

The wrinkles deepened round his eyes. "I've brought you some pictures, if you'd like them. For the cafe."

She looked away, not wanting to see what Simon had brought with him. Photographs of Alaska. Its vast, majestic steppes.

"The walls have just been painted," she said shortly.

To cover her confusion, she drew him inside the café. Nails stuck out from the walls, where charts hung long ago. He took a framed picture from his bag and placed it on a nail.

48

Was he making fun of her – her small-village existence – by bringing in these photos of the world beyond?

She turned her back while he put up the rest.

"What do you think, Cate?"

It was the tone he'd used before, when he'd shown her a photograph. Uncertain. As though it really mattered, what she thought.

She twisted. The scruffy room had vanished. Instead, swans, ducks, waders, even an otter, burst out from the walls.

"For you. From me and the wetlands. For the Boatyard Café."

Simon's eyes, Cate learnt when she looked into them at last, were green. She'd never thought she'd stare into eyes that were not Adam's, and glimpse in them a future. How had she denied herself so long this wondrous, intense green?

"I thought you were staying in Alaska."

He looked out at the languid, muddied river. "I couldn't stay away."

DANCING IN THE GRASS

June 2018, and the ecological apocalypse was taking hold. Extinctions were on the rise, insects in decline. Scientists were warning that a pandemic was on the cards.

If all this was really happening, the chalk grasslands hadn't heard. The grasses were high that summer, rollicking in the wind. Amongst them all were slender, pinkish spikes: orchids, in numbers I had never seen before.

That's what I told Agata, when I met her by chance that summer morning, on the corner that gave on to the down.

"Orchids? Real?" she said.

Crickets whirred, drowning out the traffic.

"I can show you, if you like?"

She paused: long enough to remind me that we were not friends.

"Yes. All right. You show me."

I glanced down at her canvas lace-up shoes – white, the kind we'd once called plimsols – hoping they could withstand the muddied paths. My dog, Hera, wove about her knees.

Then, together, we stepped on to the down: the great expanse of waving grassland, sweet-scented, opening before us; so we became explorers, poised upon its edge. Far to the east rose the far-off towers of London.

"You've been here before?" I asked.

Her eyes, outlined in turquoise, blinked. "Yes. Sometimes."

51

"You haven't seen the orchids?"

"No."

"I'll show you. Over here, I think."

My voice came false and forced, the walk that I had planned – just me and Hera – slipping from my grasp. I struck off on a path that sloped diagonally down. Grass-heads danced around us, russet, pink and gold. Orchids could be hard to find. Some days I searched for them in vain, in places I was certain that they grew; only to stumble on them by chance, in other spots entirely.

A pair of skylarks rose and fell, on separate strings, cascading down their song. I tried to catch Agata's eye, to share the joyous sound. She did not look at me. A yellow bag hung from her shoulder: a bag I recognised, for it stood on my hall table, on days she came to clean.

"We'll find them soon," I said.

Ahead, Hera ran and tumbled with another dog. I loved her wild bounds through the grass, her small head rising like a meerkat's to check on where I was. Behind her, I caught a glimpse of pink.

"Look – over here –"

And yes – a cluster of exquisite blooms, each pale, lobed flower freckled with magenta. Common spotted orchids: the kind that grew most widely on the down. I beckoned Agata closer.

She crouched a little distance from me. "This is – orchid?"

"Beautiful, aren't they? They grow here because the ground is chalk."

A butterfly flapped past my cheek. They were meadow browns that week, as I recall.

"Is not orchid."

"Well — yes, it is," I said.

"No. Is not."

"It's not?"

I began to wish I had not met Agata, nor asked her, in some misplaced, friendly impulse, to join me on the down. She straightened, white face turned.

"You mean — it's not like the orchids in the shops?"

A tiny nod.

Understanding made me want to laugh out loud. I pictured the fat, white, arching blooms, for sale in every supermarket. No wonder she was disappointed, when those were the flowers she had pictured in her head.

"But these are wild orchids, Agata. They're native, smaller. It's just the way they are."

"Is all?" she asked.

"Yes — well, we may see pyramidal orchids too. They're a brighter pink, more spectacular in a way," I blustered. More and more, I longed to walk alone. Instead, pushing to my feet, I said: "We can look for those too, if you like?"

A sigh, as though she, too, were being polite.

"Okay."

I called for Hera, more sharply than was normal, and changed to another path. We were reaching the bottom of the down, where the grass gave way to trees and brambles and, beyond, houses, newly built. Along this unkempt edge, a smattering of orchids grew. Find one quickly, I thought, and head away.

From behind me came an exclamation: "Look!"

I turned. Agata was kneeling beside a group that I had missed: pyramidal orchids, vibrant, fuchsia-pink, each bloom a ballerina's skirt.

"Beautiful." She ran a varnished nail along a flower.

Of course: the thrill lay in discovery. She had not needed me to show her, but to find them for herself.

Caught up in her delight, I stepped towards her. As I did so, her hand twisted and –

"Stop," I gasped.

She sat back on her heels.

"Agata – I'm sorry – you can't pick them. These orchids are wild. They're protected. It's illegal –"

She got up, brushing dust from her washed-out jeans. "Not pick?"

"No. You absolutely can't –"

"In my country –"

"This is England. Wildflowers are protected here."

My voice flared louder than I wished. The outcome of the vote was known by then. England – Britain – weren't words that I said easily. Agata was applying for residency, she'd said, though she wasn't sure if she would get it. I'd wondered if she'd ask for help, for proof of the years she'd worked for me, three hours a week, cash left on the shelf. She hadn't, and I hadn't offered.

"In my country –"

"This isn't your country."

A couple walking on the down looked across at us. Agata's eyes were dark. The orchid lay between us, slumped and bruised.

"I'm sorry," I said, to the girl who scrubbed my toilets, swept my floors. "It's just I care about the down."

A noise came to my left: Hera, collar jangling, was rushing back towards us. I stretched my hand as she surged past, relishing her taut-thighed strength. Then, beside me, I noticed something else. Something that unfolded at the far edge of my vision. A movement that, by the time I saw it, could not be prevented: Agata falling backwards, a slow-motion toppling, and gentle crumpling, down to the cushion of the grass.

"Are you alright?"

She lay there, still.

"Agata — are you alright?"

Her eyelids fluttered.

"My goodness — did Hera push you?"

She did not move. The dog stood near us, head held low. I pictured Agata unlocking my front door, Hera leaping round her in delight. A cool breeze blew.

Her hand crept to her face. She dashed some small speck from her cheek. Then, slowly, she sat up. Her bag had fallen and I retrieved it. She got up to her feet.

"Agata, are you alright? I'm so sorry if — Hera didn't mean it, you know how much she loves you —"

The girl — woman, now I looked at her, for there were fine lines on her forehead — seemed to shudder. Then she grasped hold of her right wrist. Her eyes were a deep grey-blue, a colour that before I had not noticed.

"Is broken, I think."

"Broken? What is broken?"

"My wrist." She held it out. "I cannot bend."

"Are you sure? Please, let me see —"

"No." She stepped away. "Am sorry. Cannot work." She looked up to the corner of the down. "You will have to pay."

Pay?

"Hera," I called, my voice high. "Come here."

She came at once, pushing her nose against my hand as I clicked the lead on to her collar.

"Agata — we must get you to a doctor —"

"Broken wrist — no work."

I smiled stupidly.

"Will need lawyer."

Lawyer?

"If it's broken, I must take you to the hospital," I said.

"No. I go now. Thank you for showing flowers."

"But Agata — if your wrist is broken — you need help. You need an X-ray. I can take you —"

"Is no need," she interrupted. "I go."

She turned away, her right wrist cradled. I watched her walk back up the down, towards the road. At any minute, the game would end. A few steps on — when she thought I was not looking — her hand would fall back to her side. I stood, shading my eyes against the sun. Agata trudged towards the corner, her right arm clasped against her body. Then she stepped on to the road and vanished from my sight.

"She was teasing you," my husband said that evening, when I told him what had happened. "She'll be back on Monday, right as rain. We're her livelihood, remember?"

On Sunday evening I tidied the house as usual and put her money on the high shelf in the kitchen. At 8am next day, the time her key turned in the lock, my phone pinged. A text. I hunted for my glasses.

"Wrist broken. Cannot work. You get letter."

I phoned my husband, who was on the train.

"She's bluffing," he said. "Don't give into it. Nothing will come of it, you'll see."

Next day, a thud at the front door. A thick white envelope, lying on the mat.

'Dear Mrs Graham, Our client has been involved in an accident for which you are responsible.'

The name on the letterhead was a solicitor's that I had never heard of.

'As owner of the dog, you are liable for compensation and our client's loss of earnings.'

"I'm not even sure that Hera made her fall," I told my husband at his office. "Maybe she just lost her footing."

"Ignore it. They're ambulance chasers. She probably wrote that letter herself."

I googled the law firm on the letterhead. It had no address that I could find; only a website, promising large sums for mishaps of all kinds. I tried not to dwell on what had happened, as my husband wished. We had different views on many things, these days.

With Hera, I walked along the down as the orchids browned and sank into the sward. Back home, without Agata, crumbs lurked in the corners of the work-tops. Woodlice stalked the floors.

Another letter, supplying further details. 'Our client, Ms Kaminski' – was that her name? I had forgotten – 'requires £50,000 for loss of earnings and £50,000 for the injury to her wrist.'

"£100,000?" I told my husband. "But that's impossible. That's far more than she earns a year. I don't know if Hera pushed her anyway. She might have fallen by herself."

My husband looked like he was losing patience. "I've said before, ignore it. She's threatening you. Any more and we'll go to the police."

I walked each day with Hera, longer walks that took us across the down to the woods and fields beyond. My eyes still searched for dots of pink; but, when I found them, they were vetches, threading through the grass. The meadow browns had given way to tortoiseshells. I barely saw them as they fluttered past.

Another week, another letter. I must pay now or face more penalties. £500,000 was mentioned.

I folded the stiff paper and put it in a drawer. I was sleeping badly, dreaming of falling and being chased. My skin itched. I argued with my husband, about matters of all kinds. I wondered whether, without telling him, I should get legal advice myself.

One morning as I left our gate, a child on a scooter came racing down towards me. He was a boy of three or four, his face lit up with the joy of speed. Smiling, I stepped aside to let him pass. A woman ran beside him, grasping the scooter's handle. She was young and slim and laughing as she ran. It was a game I had played with my sons too: pretending to run faster, while trying to slow them down.

I shortened Hera's lead as the pair drew close. The boy was shouting in a language I did not know. He and his mother wore hooded coats, for the mornings were cold by then. They passed and the woman's eyes – a deep blue-grey – latched on to mine.

She hurried on. The boy half-turned, unbalancing the scooter. The woman spoke sharply. My phone was in my hand. I pressed the button on its camera, over and over, as the pair glanced back once more, then sped off down the street.

Our walk was short that day. Back home, I scrutinised my pictures. Zooming in, I saw things I had missed. The boy's concentration. His mother's tight, pale jeans. The sunny yellow of her bag. I scrolled through quickly. Then something else – the woman's face, caught in the moment she looked back. The flushed face of a mother running, trying to keep up. Agata, bursting with health and energy. Her wrist, unhurt.

I made strong coffee and drank it fast. Then I tugged open the cupboard beneath the sink. Inside were cleaning fluids of all kinds; stained cloths and dusters; unmatched rubber gloves. The mess of it surprised me: this was her domain, not mine. I threw out empty bottles and stiffened, dried out cloths.

Then I began to vacuum, dust, brush and scrub. Three hours, I discovered, were not enough to clean a house. How had she done it? For one, two, three hours longer, I swept cobwebs from the ceilings and dust from beneath the beds. Coughing, I threw open windows. Then, head aching from the chemicals, I limped into the shower.

Agata: I pictured her as she had arrived, so often, at my door. The canvas lace-up shoes, the belted jacket, the bag that was not leather. Her face, so perfectly made up. The vibrant nails. The son, just three or four, I did not know she had.

Clean, I rifled through my wardrobe. A dress; not sagging jeans and jumper, as she was used to seeing me. Foundation. Blusher. A line of blue along my lashes, the way that she did hers. Not the woman Agata met when she arrived each Monday. The woman who fretted about wildflowers, and paid her by the hour.

In quiet corners of the down, I parted the myriad tiny stems in search of lady's-tresses. A pale, honey-scented orchid, difficult to spot; named for its appearance, like a plait of hair, coiling down a woman's back. A flower of the chalk, appearing at the end of summer, on ground long left unfertilised. A plant I had seen just once or twice, in places I had told no one.

For hours and days I searched, in fields ever further from my home. At last I knelt before it: a single, perfect bloom.

The address was on the scrap of paper she had passed me when we met. I found it, slipped into a drawer. In less than twenty minutes I was there: a big old house, neglected, on the other side of town. Sheets drying in the front garden; rows of buzzers lined up by the door. No name I knew among them. Turning, thinking I had not found her, I glimpsed a lower, basement door. A few dark steps led down to it. A scooter, slung across them.

The cheque-book in my pocket pushed against my thigh.

Smoothing my hair, I pressed the bell. A scuffling, then a silence. Inside, a person waited. I rang again. A creak, as bolts drew back. The strong, clean scent of drying clothes washed over me. I faced Agata and her son: a rare and wilting orchid thrust out in my palm.

HERE'S TO YOU, MRS AVERY

She sat down on the bed, trying to remember. Something about the day ahead was different. Something that niggled in her mind, the way the metal fastening of her skirt jagged into her back.

She tugged her cardigan lower on her hips. For years it had been her favourite, the wonderful soft cashmere bought on a trip with Mike to – Ullapool, it must have been. Silver buttons. An exquisite deep green, the colour of pine needles. And Mike had let her have it, despite the price, for cashmere had been special then, something to drive the length of the country for, to feel against her cheek.

Ruined now, of course. Not from wear, for Scottish cashmere did last forever, just as she had promised Mike, in the little shop beside the loch. Who would have thought, then, that that lovely cardigan would end up stiff and matted, boil washed, no good to anyone, with her own name, 'Avery', scrawled in ink upon the label?

Breakfast: had she had it? Hard to remember, in this unfathomable place. Breakfast: the best meal of the day, Mike used to say, though for years she had contented herself with just an apple.

Had she or hadn't she? She checked her front for crumbs. No sign of a tray, though sometimes they were collected without her knowing. She was not hungry, but that meant nothing. Why did no one tell you, when you were young, to relish the urge to eat? And hungry she had been – ravenous

— rushing in from the cold and cramming warm bread into her mouth, scrumping fruit, maddened by her need for food.

And now? Never. She could sit all day in her small square room, eating nothing, and not notice.

She swiped one curtain sideways, then the other. What was it about today that made it special? The garden lay below her — how lucky she had been, they told her, to get this view. She could see the branches of the taller shrubs, the philadelphus and amelanchier, knitting together against the whiteness of the sky: names she somehow still remembered, while other, more useful ones, were gone.

She picked up her looking glass and held it to her face. An instinctive movement, for she had been — and could say it, now she was no longer — a beautiful woman. Not many girls — and again, she could say it now — had been as lucky as she, with her raven curls and Cupid's bow. She had looked like a film star, and had longed to be one: holding up this very mirror, posturing, believing she had a chance.

And now — well, she was in her eighties. Eighty-three, not counting the four or five stray years she had knocked off long ago. An old lady, whichever way you looked at it. That was what Julie, who did breakfasts, and Selma, who did teas, saw when they blustered in to see her. Patricia Avery: nice enough, forgetful, won't be with us long. Not the Patricia Avery she had been and still remained inside: a woman who could break a hundred hearts, just by walking down a street. "But I am that person," she longed to say, to Julie and the rest. "I'm here! I haven't really changed!"

Through habit, for there was nothing there to please her now, she looked into the glass. A movement, an outline of a form: not herself, but Mike. What was he doing there? He was standing sideways to her, white hair blown across his

62

pate.

"Mike!" The name burst from her. He was speaking to someone she could not see. She moved the mirror, trying to peer behind him. A glimpse of blue – water – and yes, that little shop with the sun shining on it and the metal roof, corrugated, so thickly grown with moss it was a landscape in itself. Ullapool. There was the woman, smiling across the counter – so graceful, those Scots, so long as you did not cross them. And she herself, in that belted dress she lost sight of long ago, holding the cardigan in her arms as though it were a precious animal.

And Mike not happy, that was evident, by the sagging of his shoulders. Not happy, for the cardigan was expensive: more than they could afford. The woman gazing at him. And she, Pat, gazing at him too, wanting that cardigan more than anything. And Mike knowing this, for she could see him wilting further, beneath the combined yearning of herself and the woman, who even now was preparing to wrap the feather-light wool in saffron tissue, that only emphasised the perfection of the green.

"Patricia? Penny for them, dear?"

She put the mirror down.

Julie's busy presence filled the room. A clank as the breakfast tray landed on the bedside table.

"Cup of tea, dear?"

She twisted towards the voice. Julie: pink, cheerful, bringer of breakfasts, harbinger of another day. Only – who was this? Mouth hidden; masked like an intruder, or a dog that had been muzzled. Not pink, friendly Julie. A different, terser version, who did not stay to chat.

"Yes, please." Her own voice, thin with shock.

"In your chair?"

"Yes."

"There you are, dear. Eat up for your big day."

Big day? She peered down on the tray. Boiled egg, a tiny glass of orange juice, a cup of greyish tea. Perhaps, at some unremembered time, she had ticked a box agreeing this would be her breakfast, every day; just as she had seemed to tick another box, permitting the world to call her by her Christian name.

"I am not Patricia, apart from to my dearest, oldest friends," she thought. "I am Mrs Avery, and I'll thank you to remember it."

She did not say it. Instead: "Thank you," she murmured, as the pink shape backed out through the door.

She would eat later. Instead, with the same habitual gesture, she lifted the mirror back before her face.

And what was that? A mass of movement, of childish arms and legs, hair of all shades blowing in the wind; herself in the middle, laughing, half-winded by the mayhem and excitement. Granny Pat: a role she had played to perfection.

Memories of the day came back to her. A birthday, perhaps, when all the family had come together, and she had made lunch – roast beef for everyone, that had been a strain – and then afterwards they had gone outside, to sit on the veranda. How grateful she had been, to stretch out on a lounger, a glass of something in her hand. But the children had called for her, and she had gone to them, their fairy grandmother, to stand in their circle while they whooped and danced around her.

The grandchildren: how she had loved them. Girls, most of them, who loved sifting through her pretty things, the piles of beaded evening bags and scarves. Girls who had gazed, enraptured, at photographs of her and Mike in evening dress; or her alone, on a beach, limbs oiled, like someone in a magazine.

She put the mirror down. How close she had felt to those children, delighting in their confidences, trying not to laugh. Shining in their innocence and adoration. And now? Now they did not come. Now no one came, and had not come for months: not grandchildren, nor daughters, nor Mike – though Mike could not come, for he was not alive – nor anyone she had befriended in her long years of living in the town.

Voices reached her from the corridor; not passing, as she expected, but pausing, as though the people they belonged to were huddled just outside.

The door swung open. A tall woman, see-through plastic curved around her face. Not Julie, not Selma. Not a regular at all, but surely Mrs Garland, who had not stepped into her room since the day she had arrived. Mrs Garland, manager of the home, who even now was shaking her head at the untouched tray. "Eat up, Mrs Avery. It's not every day that you make history."

What history do you mean, Patricia tried to ask; but had not time to say it, before the upright figure swished out through the door.

As it shut, she saw Mike's face, reflecting from the paintwork. Mike, looking out at her, holding their new-born child. Bella: so sweet and soft. 'Bella': the name she had demanded they should choose. Beautiful, it meant, and beautiful the child had been, though strangely she had never cared. She had grown up tall and gangly, bookish, smitten with her father; not the daughter she had hoped for, to help her in the house.

After that had come Diana, the hunter. Diana had been the one she had cleaved to most: wiry and determined, with hair as tight-curled as her own. And finally Rosemary, for remembrance, the girl they had not wanted to grow up.

No boy, of course. And that had been a problem, for Mike would have liked a boy. He was working hard by then, building up the business, closed off in his workshop. Injection moulding, a process she did not understand. Plastic shapes, whose use she did not know. A boy could have learnt all that, but not a girl. That they had agreed on. The girls had gone off to the convent for their schooling, then to Switzerland. And then they had come back, to marry in their turn.

She had felt lucky to have girls, and yet in different ways they had rejected her. Bella, the eldest, most of all. Bella, who never seemed to bother how she looked. Bella, who had met a man they knew was trouble and – though she, Patricia, had warned against him – had married him nonetheless, bringing trouble to them all.

"Come along now, Mrs A. Oh, you do look nice today. All ready for your big day?"

More voices, bodies, jostling into her room. Kind, practised hands – the sort that did not take resistance – loading her into a wheel-chair. Then out into the corridor, walls and pictures rushing past. The shush of wheels on carpet. Doors parting. Stop! Where are we going? A laugh above her head. "Just a short drive. You're a little bit of history, Mrs A."

Moving, gazing out; another scene appearing in her head. Her own mother, sitting weeping. A silent weeping, that continued, unrelenting, as each exercise book was examined, corrected, and laid upon the pile. Her brother, Henry, stretched out, fiddling with his stamps. She herself, standing by, aghast.

Their father dead – dead by then at least a decade; their mother's colossal grief still unremitting. Her mother, back working as a school teacher, now she was a widow. Always busy, always tired. Henry older, cutting himself off. And she herself, so lovely, so desirable – she saw it daily in men's faces – and yet unsure. What could she do with herself? Not clever, particularly, but full of life. Full of laughter and fun and a terrible giggling silliness that spilled over with her friends. A laughter and a silliness she could not show at home.

How to get out of there? It was not much later that men began to hang around; men from the church and other places, men who were unmarried or simply could not stop themselves. Younger men too, whom she did not know or trust. And Mike – Michael, as she had called him then. Serious. Thoughtful. Brown wavy hair, a touch receding. A pleasant, gentle face.

He took her in a punt along the Thames, while she gazed up at him, her mother decorous in the prow. And then she had married him, in a dress that was mauve, not white. A choice she had regretted afterwards, and only proved that she was foolish. Her brother frowning, as he led her down the aisle.

"We're here now, Mrs A."

More hands, ladling her out, out of the van or ambulance, out into the cold. Then in through spreading doors, along a corridor, wide and empty, smelling of disinfectant. A place that could only be a hospital. She took a breath. The world beyond already far away. A strangeness in her chest, as though a fly or moth had stolen into it and fluttered in the space between her ribs. Was she here for some scan or other? To check some troublesome, worn-out part she could not quite remember?

When she looked up next, a face was poised above her. Handsome: she took that in at once, with eyes that shimmered with feeling and concern. Eyes that were blue, above a mask of another, paler blue: the colour of – speedwell, that was it, the spreading plant that threaded though the lawn of their first house. Mike. Her dry lips parted. He had come for her at last.

"Just a sharp scratch, Mrs Avery."

He was strangely dressed, in sheets of crinkling plastic, not like Mike at all. For comfort she sought the steady blueness of his eyes: thirsting for them, more strongly than for any drink. Eyes that, as he pushed the needle into the loose flesh of her arm, seemed suddenly to well with tears.

"Don't cry, Mike," she found herself saying, as the eyes shone more brightly still. 'Try not to worry. Things will turn out for the best.'

He stared back, as though acknowledging this, their private truth.

Then, too soon, he sighed and looked away, the bliss of their togetherness broken. A swab of cotton wool pushed against her mottled skin.

"All done now, Mrs Avery. I hope that you stay well."

Her chair was gripped and wheeled around. She protested, holding out her arms, wishing to stay longer with this man who looked like Mike, and perhaps had even been him: a thing she would know for certain if only they had let her stay.

But what was this? People standing, in the corridor that before had been quite empty. Standing, waiting, chattering, raising their arms to her as though in friendly greeting. Men and women, some in uniform – nurses, surely, and doctors

68

too – tired eyes widening above their masks, lifting their hands as she approached and clapping – clapping? Surely not clapping her?

And yet it seemed they were. Clapping, yes, and cheering, and pointing cameras, for bright lights flashed into her eyes. People who wished her well. People who loved her – yes, she did not imagine it, love shone in their eyes, and tears, adding to that love, combining with the clapping, that did not die away as she drew close, but built to a crescendo.

"History": the word was whispered as she passed.

Somehow, these people knew her for who she really was. Not poor old Mrs A, fraying at the seams, forgetful and forgotten; but Patricia Avery, dazzling, mesmerising, the star she should have been.

Patricia Avery: the first to get the vaccine. First in the hospital, the town, the county: it did not matter which. First, for all she knew, in the country or the world. Patricia Avery, a name now synonymous with hope. Patricia Avery who, when the microphone is thrust towards her, can say, to these people who look like Mike, and their daughters, and Henry, her brother, and her mother too – and there, over there, surely she can see her father; can say, with the wisdom that comes only with a life-time: "Please, do not worry. Things will get better. Believe me: one day, not too far off, everything will be alright."

A STRANGE CASE OF THE RAILWAY MADNESS

The woman who sat in the corner of the railway carriage with her eyes shut was attracting a good deal of attention.

"We must give her smelling salts," a black-clad matron in a feathered hat exclaimed, lurching to her feet.

"The motion of the train afflicts her," spoke up a white-whiskered churchman from the far end of the carriage. He clasped his hands in prayer.

Miss Annie Bretherton, who sat opposite, saw that the slumped woman's face was deathly pale. Brown ringlets, slightly damp, clung to her cheeks. Her lips – which, even in her incommoded state, were redder than seemed natural – were parted and curved up.

"We must find a doctor," exclaimed the young man who had joined the train a short while back at Hanwell, stowing his top-hat on the rack above Annie's head.

Opening the door of the compartment, he rushed into the corridor.

"A doctor, is anyone a doctor?" his voice rang out, as the great steam-train thundered on.

Annie, having no medical skills to speak of, remained in her seat and observed the woman closely.

She appeared neither young nor old: around thirty, Annie supposed. Her dress, in a vivid shade of green, was fashionably cut, revealing the trimness of her waist; though its stuff was perhaps not of the highest quality. Her reverie was deep; for her eyes remained closed, while the churchman fanned his copy of *The Times* beneath her nose.

What reason could she have to be travelling, alone, out of London? Would a respectable lady even do such a thing, Annie wondered; remembering that, of course, she was doing the very same herself: heading, without a chaperone, to join the new ladies' college, Somerville Hall, just opened up at Oxford.

She ran her hand across the carpet bag behind her knees, which contained her academic books and three warm frocks, recently retrimmed. If her brothers called her a blue stocking – well, it did not matter. The year, 1879, would be remembered as the date when women were, at last, admitted to the University. By the greatest of good fortune, she, Miss Annie Bretherton of Queen's Park, was among them. If anyone in the carriage deserved attention, it was surely she herself. Had she not been specially selected, for the quickness and potential of her brain?

"Doctor coming through: what seems to be the trouble?"

A whiskered man in a tweed coat bowled through the carriage door, clasping a chestnut leather case. The train jolted, throwing him forward, almost on to Annie's lap.

"Beg your pardon, young lady."

Regaining his footing, he advanced towards the woman in the corner. A whiff of whisky and pipe smoke lingered in his wake; and Annie felt a stab of pity for the woman, who must endure his ministrations at close hand.

"Here is the patient, doctor," said the young man from Hanwell, entering behind him, gesturing to the woman in the corner.

She sat, leant back in her seat, eyes still tightly closed.

Her posture had sunk lower, as though only her position in the corner saved her from slipping to the floor. Moving to sit beside her, the doctor unclipped his leather case with a snap.

Inside, Annie glimpsed an array of small glass vials, filled with coloured fluids of all kinds.

Reassured, she watched from the corner of her eye as the doctor grasped the woman's slender wrist. Gravely, he felt for her pulse; while all present in the carriage took special interest in the fields and woods beyond.

The doctor cleared his throat. "The patient must lie down."

"Of course, the poor dear soul." The black-clad lady who had requested smelling salts clambered to her feet. Nodding thanks, the doctor gently lifted the prostrate woman's legs so she lay along the seat; then looked across at Annie.

"Your bag, if you please, Miss: for a pillow."

Certainly not, Annie thought. My precious books!

The doctor stretched out his hand. Faces turned towards her, as though to say: "Do your duty, Miss, and assist this helpless lady."

With ill grace, Annie heaved her bag up and passed it to the doctor, who placed it beneath the woman's lolling head.

"What is your diagnosis, Doctor?" the churchman asked.

"It is hard to say precisely. I will fix a tonic for her. In fifteen minutes, I may know more."

"Should we stop the train?" asked the young man from Hanwell.

"I believe that would not help her, sir; since we are in the country, where the only living things around are sheep and cows."

"The guard may assist us," the young man suggested.

The doctor frowned. "Do not fret, sir. All is under my control."

At the University, Annie would surely meet men like the doctor: learned and confident in their powers. Legs braced against the movement of the train, he dripped fluids from one vial to the next, shaking and inspecting them against the light. Annie thought of academic papers she had read, surreptitiously, on her brother Norton's desk. Norton, now a doctor at St Bart's, took an interest not just in the body, but also in the mind. One article in particular had caught Annie's eye. It cited the case of daily-breaders – men who travelled by train each day for their work – who, without warning, acted strangely. One had taken off his clothes and run naked through the train. Another had unsheathed a knife and stabbed a fellow passenger to death. The paper suggested that, in certain character types, the train's unnatural, throbbing motion produced undesirable effects. Perhaps, Annie thought – as steam billowed past the window and the pistons pumped and pounded – the woman in her carriage might be afflicted in a similar way.

If so, Annie would observe the woman closely, for an interest in the connections between the body and the mind underpinned her wish to study. True, her father – believing all books beyond the Bible did harm to a woman's brain – had compelled her to read Theology. But once she had arrived at the great University, how could he stop her? She would have access to the finest libraries, where books were held in place by chains. She would make cases such as this her private course of study: to discuss with Norton, when she came home.

"How can we thank you, doctor?" the lady clad in black

was saying, as the doctor tilted back the recumbent woman's head and dripped blue liquid past her lips.

"Five minutes," he intoned. "Then we will know her fate."

"Five minutes," the whisper crept around the carriage.

Five minutes, Annie thought, looking at her pocket-watch. In five minutes, they would arrive at Slough, and the patient could be carried from the train.

Even as she thought it, the woman in the green dress gave a twitch. Her arms, then her legs, began to writhe. Her eyes, that had stayed so tightly shut, flew open. A gurgle issued from her throat.

She is seized by the railway madness, Annie thought, as the woman's pale fingers flew up to her neck and closed round her own wind-pipe. Remember every detail, Annie thought coolly, as the churchman and the man from Hanwell leapt up to their feet to tear her fragile hands away. Annie imagined how later, at the University, she might present her account: 'The Railway Madness: A Small Case Study'. An academic paper that perhaps would make her name.

"Aaaaaagghhhhh!"

The woman's deathly scream filled the carriage.

All present crowded round her, talking at once, hands fluttering in their concern and distress.

Only the doctor stood back, behind the worried onlookers. His hands too, Annie saw, had begun to flutter. Was it her imagination, or were his fingers darting forward? Dipping, even, into pockets; extracting whatever they contained and, with a brisk movement, depositing them into his own capacious coat? Before she could make sense of what she saw, or utter any warning, the doctor flung down the window. Blasting its horn, the train slid into Slough. Amid the screech of brakes and hiss of steam, the man began to hurl things from the carriage. Out went the black-clad lady's suitcase, the churchman's bag, even the hat that belonged to the pleasant-looking man from Hanwell.

A man in a black waist-coat ran beside the train; catching every object and stowing them on to a makeshift trolley.

Stretched out on the seat, the ailing woman groaned and clutched her throat. Only very slowly, so great was their compassion for her, did Annie's fellow passengers become aware that their possessions – bags, purses, wallets, scarves – were missing. As they checked the racks and seats, slapping their pockets in confusion, the woman in the green dress sat bolt upright. The corners of her reddened lips curled higher. Taking Annie's carpet bag, on which her head had rested, she launched it from the window of the train.

The bag flew high into the air.

The running man outside the train, lengthening his stride, caught it in his arms. When the train was fully stopped, she would thank him and retrieve it.

Though the train moved dangerously fast, the doctor was wresting the door open. As it swung back, he held his arm out to the woman in the green dress. She – miraculously restored – took hold of his hand and leapt with him from the train. The man with the trolley with the bags shouted something to them. All three sped across the platform, down a passageway and out of sight.

"Charlatans," breathed the churchman, his mouth stretched to an ugly 'O'.

"My hat," said the man from Hanwell.

"My books," Annie cried.

Aghast, she fell back to her seat. Yes, her brain was as large as any man's: that, she still believed. Yet, before even reaching her new Hall, she had learnt a useful lesson: that she was not, after all, quite as clever as she thought.

JACK'S HEDGE

She plants Jack's hedge the day he goes to war.

Hawthorn, hazel, spindle, blackthorn: saplings she finds about the farm. Plants them, in a line from the farmhouse, to the edge of the South Field.

Jack's Hedge. March, April, the shoots take root. Bright young leaves; a dust of blossom, here and there. Jack writes that he's in training, at an air base in the east.

June, he's home on leave. Hair short, a different boy from when he left. Reconnaissance, he tells her: hunched up with his camera, taking photos far below. Vital war work. Sorry, Ma, I can't say any more.

That summer, he's in action. She looks up at the silver planes skimming overhead. Is Jack there, at a window, staring down? At night, she lies rigid; old Tom peaceful at her side.

Months pass. Jack's letters, telling them he's safe.

Two summers. Then, the next July, the postman's step comes heavy. She's learnt the news already, by the poppy, that's sprung up by Jack's Hedge.

The hedge: it is her comfort. Abuzz with butterflies, beetles, hoverflies. The ceaseless throb of life.

"We must move on with the times, pet," Tom tells her, when the war is done. "Grow food for our country. It's what our Jack would want."

Would he? She remembers Jack, transfixed by a field-mouse. A boy who'd scoop an earth-worm in his hands rather than squash it with his boot.

Machines come, rip up hedgerows that have stood for centuries. In their place, wide fields she doesn't recognise; crops she doesn't know.

But Jack's Hedge keeps growing. It's an oasis, a refuge, for creatures that have lost their homes. Violets seed along it. Birds nest in the thorns.

She tends and lays its branches, takes cuttings. Soon, has enough for a new hedge.

She writes to the War Graves Commission, to ask if they'll accept the plants she's grown. A letter back: "Thank you, Mrs Stovold, but our cemeteries must look the same, in honour of the dead."

What can she do with them, instead?

Mrs Dawkins in the village, she's lost her son. Turns out she'd like a little hedge to sit by.

Ant — Jack's old best friend — he'd like one too.

The village school, it wants a garden, where children can learn about the species that are missing from the farms. She helps them plant her saplings. At the opening, tells them of the birds and insects that flit along Jack's Hedge.

She and Tom, their farm is different from the rest. More skylarks, reptiles, dragonflies. Stewardship: a word she hasn't heard of. Finds out, she's done it all along.

Tom comes one day, when she's sitting in the shade.

"Shall we go and see him, Irene? You know, before it gets too late?"

That's how, at last, in France, she sees the spot where Jack crashed down to earth. A wooden cross; beside it, hawthorn, hazel, spindle, sprouting at the field edge. Jack, at rest. His spirit, growing with the hedge.

HURRY UP AND BRUSH YOUR FEET

"Hurry up and brush your feet," Cassie said to Sam, her elder son.

He stood braced inside the door frame of the bathroom, making faces at his brother down the hall.

"I mean, brush your teeth." With luck, Sam would not notice her small slip.

His long-lashed eyes rolled upward. "What are you talking about, Mum?"

"I said, get a move on! School's starting any minute!"

Ahead loomed another day of what was called 'home schooling'. Which, while spent at home, could only in the loosest sense be billed as 'schooling'. Another day when her teenage sons would stay inside their rooms, noses stuck in laptops, switching screens if she walked in. Another day when her temper would wear thin.

A red plastic football bounced along the hallway, colliding with her shins.

"Didn't mean to, Mum," called Danny, her younger son, grinning from the doorway of his room.

As Cassie lunged for the ball, Sam slid past her and sent it spinning back towards his brother.

Danny flicked the ball up with his toe, then volleyed it towards them. The globe of cheap red plastic came spinning back, smacking Cassie in the mouth.

"Sam," she yelled in fury. "I mean, Danny. Both of you. I've had enough."

Scooping the ball up, she hurled it inside the hallway cupboard.

"Say sorry," Sam reproved his brother. His toothbrush, protruding from his mouth, clattered like an old man's pipe.

"You're both too old for this. Hurry up and brush your feet!"

Aghast at another error, Cassie stumbled to the kitchen. Brush your feet: she'd been saying it for weeks now. And, just as bad, hadn't she told Sam, just the other day, to scrub his dirty teeth? Feet, teeth. Teeth, feet. Words that in some recess of her brain were interchanged, though she knew the instant she pronounced them they were wrong.

She was tired, that was all. Leaning on the work-top, Cassie jammed the kettle on to boil.

Around her, the thin walls shook as her two sons traded blows. Testosterone leaked from their pores, rising in a tsunami at moments such as these: the oily fluid, that drove their teenage lives.

Sam was fourteen, Danny a year younger. By now they should be at their desks, tuned in to their lessons. Sam's recently-broken voice roared out an expletive. Sam, who always claimed she treated him unfairly: judging him more harshly than his brother.

How could she blame her sons if, penned in a small flat, their hormones sometimes overflowed? It wasn't right for boys their age to be at home, cut off from their friends. Schools closed, sports and clubs on hold. Cooped up with their mother, worst of all.

The kettle clicked and she poured water into her mug, clamping the tea-bag against its side. As she flicked the bag towards the bin, a coppery juice dripped across the counter.

Cassie stared. A poisonous ore – not so different from the streak along the work-top – ran down through her family: seeping through the generations, along the female line. Her great grandmother, grandmother, distant aunts: all, sooner or later, began to fumble with their words. Her mother too, when Cassie was in her teens, had lost the power of speech, like water gurgling down a drain.

Dementia. Alzheimer's. Call it what you like, the condition was embedded in them: mangled letters in a stick of sea-side rock.

Now, though she was not yet 45, it had come for her.

Cassie remembered her own mother, driving her crazy with her dippy inability to remember words and names. Followed, with alarming speed, by the loss of her ability to speak, walk, feed herself or recognise those around her.

Not that Cassie had stuck around to see. Sensing what was to come, she had dropped out from her nursing course – the irony of that did not strike her until later – and gone to work on cruise ships, a boarding school in Inverness and, finally, an ashram. By the time she came home, her mother was dead; her father and brother too hurt by her long absence to welcome her back into their lives.

Her sons' shouts and thumps were growing louder. Would things be different if Kelvin had not checked out of their lives? She imagined saying, "Oh, go and sort them out," and her ex-husband's bulk restoring order, as she herself could not. Was that what teenage boys required: a father, heavier than they were, to outface them?

"School time," she bawled into the hall.

The noises dwindled. Cassie guessed they were settling at their laptops, registering at their lessons; soon slipping off, to YouTube and online games. Boys she could not discipline: for why should they respect a mother who spoke nonsense, as though a mischief-making gremlin in her brain was switching all the points?

Go to Dr Priyah, Cassie thought, as she sat and sipped her tea. Dr Priyah, their family GP, with her searching gaze and friendly manner. For years, Cassie had taken the boys to her, waiting while Dr Priyah probed and questioned; only to announce that what was needed was not some dramatic intervention, but, in fact, a big fat nothing.

Which was, Cassie sometimes thought, the best a cash-strapped health service could provide. Still, Dr Priyah's diagnoses had proved correct. So much so that 'a big fat nothing' had become a catch-phrase, that they had laughed at, at the time.

Kindly Dr Priyah. But how could Cassie bother her now? Now, when people were dying, ambulances wailing, infection rates higher by the day? How could she take up Dr Priyah's time, on a problem so small and insignificant as mixing up her words?

The doorbell buzzed. Scraping back her chair, Cassie hurried down the concrete stairs. A cardboard box waited in the stairwell. Guessing the delivery man had pushed all the bells and left, she checked whom the box was for. Cassie Jackson, her own name, was on the label. Odd, when she had ordered nothing.

She carried the box upstairs. Perhaps one of her sons had bought something online and used her credit card to pay. Sam had done so once or twice without telling her.

In the kitchen, she washed her hands, then slit the thick grey plastic tape. Inside the box was another that seemed, from its picture, to contain a kettle.

84

What did she want with a kettle? Non-plussed, she drew it from its polystyrene sleeves. Heavier than her own, with an expensive-looking matt-silver finish, it resembled a kettle she'd seen at her friend Wendy's, which flipped on a blue light as it boiled. She'd admired it at the time. But not enough to buy one.

She remembered, as a young woman, going home for a rare visit. In her old bedroom, scarcely touched, she opened the wardrobe to see what clothes she'd left behind. A thin, solid packet fell out at her feet. Other packets followed, like a poorly-built brick wall, collapsing. Each was wrapped in clear, sharp-cornered plastic. Inside were duvet covers, pillow cases, fitted sheets – all new and unopened. Bought by their mother, her brother told her later: purchases she could not remember making, too many to be sorted and returned.

Hands cupped round her mug, Cassie considered the new kettle, whose curving silver surface now seemed full of menace. Had she really ordered it, and not remembered? In which case, were other kettles on their way, that she'd bought and then forgotten, like her mum?

She must send the kettle back, before Sam and Danny asked why it was there. Didn't she tell them, every week, she didn't have spare cash for the football shirts and trainers they demanded?

Everyone bought things online and then forgot, Cassie told herself, as she packed the kettle up. Weren't charity shops full of gadgets in their boxes, and clothes with their labels still attached? The big Tesco on the far side of the town had a Post Office counter. The rules said she could go out once a day, for essentials. She'd return the kettle, without the boys even knowing she had gone.

The shop's bright white aisles were almost empty. The woman at the Post Office accepted the repackaged box without question. What had Cassie expected: to be scrutinised and asked if she were going mad? She bought pizzas for the boys' supper and a bag of salad, then walked back to her car.

Her key did not fit in the car door. She tried again, wiggling the key slightly, for the lock was prone to rusting after rain. The key refused to turn. Taking it out, she wiped it on her jeans, then inserted it more carefully. The key stuck, as before. A muscled man in a white T-shirt, pushing his filled trolley, paused to watch. Cassie smiled, to show she was not a car thief. Bottles clanking, the man moved on. Rain began to fall. Setting her carrier bag of pizzas against a spindly tree, losing its fight for life amid a sea of tarmac, Cassie hunkered by her car. "Come on," she hissed, willing the key to turn.

"Can I help?"

A young man in a shiny suit stood beside her. Estate agent, by the look of him. They were still working, weren't they, while everyone else was stuck at home?

"I'm trying to unlock my car."

Perhaps the man would help, though he didn't look the mechanical type.

"My car, actually."

"What?"

He took a key from his pocket and dangled it before her. "This is my car. Look."

Inserting his own key, he turned it without effort. The locks inside the car clicked up.

"Oh – I'm sorry –"

Cassie backed away. Would he be angry, thinking she'd been trying to steal his car?

86

He gazed around the car park. "Look, there's another red Panda over there —"

Looking where he pointed, Cassie saw a car unmistakeably her own — rusted round the doors, with a dent on the left bumper — parked in the next row down.

She tapped her head. "Silly me —"

"Easy mistake," the young man said pleasantly. "Have a good day."

Safe inside her car, Cassie bent her head. Hadn't her mother had mishaps, scarcely different, when Cassie and her brother were young? She remembered the day they'd left their small village and driven to Plymouth. Later, they'd walked for hours on endless, uphill streets while their mother tried to find the car. In the end, she had flagged a taxi and they drove about, all three craning from the windows, Cassie gnawing at her nails in shame. At last, her brother spotted their white Rover. On the way home, their mother missed the turn-off to their village. Soon after that, she gave up driving for good.

Back home, Cassie thrust the pizza boxes deep into the fridge. The house was quiet, her sons no doubt in headphones, buried in the Internet. She remembered Kelvin getting annoyed when she drove: the way she could be driving down a street she'd been a thousand times, and suddenly forget which way to turn. 'Stupid', he had called her. And stupid she had felt, until it was easier to just let Kelvin drive. Stupid, he'd called her on the day he announced that he was leaving. Was that what Sam and Danny thought of her, as well?

She drank a cup of instant coffee, then picked up the phone. Dr Priyah's number was programmed in, from the days when the boys were young. Her finger hovered, then pressed down.

A woman's voice came on the line. "Thank you for calling –"

Cassie jumped. "I'd like an appointment with Dr Priyah, please. I've got a problem you see, I can't –"

"Please be aware that the surgery is currently receiving a larger than usual number of calls," the recorded voice droned on. "You may find it quicker to go online at –"

Options washed over her. How could she choose which one, when all she wanted was to speak to Dr Priyah? Music began to play, jangly and repetitive. She listened for a few moments, then ended the call.

Finger shaking, she jabbed the radio on, then filled a glass of water.

Words. Perhaps she'd lost the knack of talking, in the months she'd sat silent, after Kelvin left. Days she hadn't gone to work, but sat on the sofa in her PJs, ignoring the ringing of the phone. Her mouth at once too empty and too full, so she could not explain to her manager that she could not come to work that day, nor tomorrow, nor the one after that. Weeks when to say "Hello," and "How was your day?" when her sons came home from school, exhausted every atom of her love.

'Uptown Girl' was blaring from the radio, a song she'd loved when she was young. Glass in hand, she began to strut around the kitchen. At school, before everyone left for better things, there'd been a talent show on the hall stage. Someone had sung 'Uptown Girl', as brilliantly as Billy Joel himself. And she, plain Caz Cox as she was then, had been the girl in the video – Christie Brinkley, that name she could remember – prancing up and down the stage, the envy of every girl in the whole school.

After that, she'd gone away to train as a nurse. In odd phone calls, wedged into a phone box with a pile of ten pence pieces, she understood that things back home were difficult. Her father evaded questions. From her brother, she absorbed not information, but resentment. Resentment that she, Cassie – her new, college name, that he couldn't bring himself to say – hadn't stuck around to help.

How could she go back, after that? Instead, haunted by a livid fear of what her mother had become, she'd kept running. By the time she was ready to come home, the mother she loved was dead.

'Uptown girl – she's been living in her uptown world –'

As she swung around, her right arm brushed the handle of the fridge. The glass she'd forgotten she was holding flew up in the air, water showering, then smashed into a shoal of glistening pieces on the floor.

Her mother, too, broke cups and glasses. Cassie's eyes grew wet, water spilling down her cheeks and neck, soaking the neckline of her T-shirt. A streak of blood edged across one knee. What should she do? On the radio, a woman was trying to guess the date a song had been released. '1996?' she tried. A klaxon blared, to show she'd got it right. How could the woman remember? Why could she recall such useless trivia, while Cassie struggled to produce the simplest words?

"Mum? Are you alright?"

Sam's voice, from the hall.

She sprang to life, pushing shards of glass along the bottom of the units where they would not be seen. Glass snagged her skin and her index finger began to bleed.

"Mum – what's going on?"

Sam, with his deep brown eyes and hair that fell into his eyes – like Kelvin's, when she'd met him – appeared inside the door.

"Nothing. I dropped a glass, that's all."

"What's happened with your hand? Look, I'll clear up. You get a plaster –"

She watched as Sam – all gangly limbs, like his father, at the start – took the dustpan from the cupboard and swept up the flecks of glass. Emptying the glass into a thick brown bag, he stuffed it in the bin.

"Are you alright, Mum? I mean, really alright?" he said, as the lid flipped shut.

She'd have to remind him to cut that silly fringe.

"Of course I'm alright." Cassie wound kitchen roll around her bleeding finger. 'There's pizza for your tea."

"It's just – Danny and I – we get the feeling something's wrong."

Sam pushed his shoulders back. It wasn't his fault he looked so like his father; with his newly deepened voice, sounded like him too.

"I mean, your words, Mum. The way you say things wrong –"

"No I don't," Cassie exploded. What would Sam say next? That she was losing her mind, not fit to be a mother? That he and Danny – well, they'd rather live with Dad now, thanks very much?

"We want to help you, Mum –"

They would not visit her, wherever she ended up. Just as she had not visited her own mother.

"Most likely, it's all fine, Mum. But if something's wrong, it's better to know sooner. I've looked it up online. There are things that can be done —"

"I'm not listening," Cassie said. She stood up, teeth clenched, chin raised to her son. Sam stepped closer, pushing the fringe back from his forehead. His face was longer than she'd noticed it before, his cheekbones high and sharp.

"Mum? While you were out — well, we rang the doctor's. Dr Priyah can see you, 8.15am on Friday. It's early but it's the only space she had. Thing is, it's before school. Me and Danny can come with you, if you like —"

"Come with me?" She searched for the mockery in his smile. Waited for a voice, not Sam's but his father's, to call her mad or stupid. "You mean — you want to help me?"

"Yes… if you don't mind?"

Her arms flung wide to embrace her elder son. Nothing like his bullying father, she understood at last. Nothing like the selfish child she'd been herself.

He hugged her back, then drew away.

"I'll get Danny — he'll want to know as well —"

Sam's steady steps faded up the hall.

91

THE TRUTH HAS ARMS AND LEGS

BERLIN, OCTOBER 1942

"Time to pack up now, Elli," Auntie says.

They are her favourite words. How many times in every day must she pronounce them? Every time I have spread my paper dolls or built my farm — why, then I must stop and clear them all away.

"Five minutes more, Auntie."

"No, Elli. This very instant."

I glance at her, under cover of moving a sheep from one field to the next. Twin spots emblazon her thin cheeks. I must do as she says or Auntie will explode: not the whizz-crash-bang of fireworks but a colder, silent fury.

I push my dolls into their paper bag, gently to preserve their limbs. Auntie moves back and forth on business of her own.

"Faster, Elli," she says, descending on me. "Pack up now. You have fifteen minutes —"

I turn back to the world of sheep and cows, for fifteen minutes lasts forever, and even Auntie knows it.

She sweeps her arm across my farm so everything collapses: fences tumbling, animals knocked on to their sides.

"I am telling you to pack up everything, Elli."

"Everything?"

With that word my existence changes. Everything is not just my farm and paper dolls. Everything includes my chess set and pack of cards and two spare nighties wedged beside the chimney. It means our jars of oats and tea, and rye bread wrapped in cloth.

"Why everything?" I ask.

"Oh, Elli," my aunt says. "Pack, for goodness' sake, and then give me a hand."

I do as she requests. She is moving faster than I have ever seen her, stiff legs striding, stuffing all we own into the two canvas bags with which we came. I add my clothes on top of hers, crushing them as she directs. There is space for my paper dolls to slide in too, bent a little but that cannot be helped. I add my farm animals on top, pushing them down so metal horns and hooves imprint into my palms.

"Take those out," she says.

"That's my farm."

She stops beside me. "You cannot take it, Elli. We have no room. I'm sorry. It will have to stay behind."

Tears come and I summon my strength to still them.

"Can I take a horse and a sheep? One sheep, one horse, one cow?"

She nods, rushing on, shoving our meagre foodstuffs into the second bag. She takes her clock from the shelf, adding it on top. I look around. The place is almost cleared. We have not many possessions, after all.

"Where are we going?" I ask, when her pace slows.

"They are letting us go," she says.

"You mean that we are free?"

"Yes, Elli. We are free."

She slips back the wooden panel behind her makeshift bed that I am not allowed to touch. We stumble out. The space beyond smells different, of wood and something I think is cheese. Trunks are stacked up in the darkness in misshapen piles. Auntie puts a finger to her lips. We shuffle to one side.

Sounds come from below, of furniture scraped on wooden floors. Auntie does not look at me. She takes my hand. I feel her skin, papery on mine.

The trapdoor rises, letting in a shaft of yellow light. Fingers appear. They are thick, man's fingers, with dark hairs above the knuckle. I hear his laboured breath. The trapdoor inches upward. Auntie tugs its little handle, while the man pushes from below.

His stubbled face appears, grey moustache just level with our feet.

"Well, Kati," he says to Auntie, as though there is nothing unusual in his position. "You know that it is time."

"It is time," she agrees, her palm pressed into mine.

"The little one," he says, and looks at me.

The hairy hands reach out. Auntie pushes, so I half-walk, half-fall into his arms. My dangling feet touch nothing. I tug my thin skirt lower. He grasps my waist and lowers me down. Different, softer arms encircle me and transport me to the floor. Auntie passes down our bags. Her thick-stockinged legs come next, wavering in mid-air. I am embarrassed at her clumsiness.

The man puts out his hand to help her. "I am sorry, Kati," he says. "There is no other way."

She nods and smiles so that, despite his words, I am reassured.

"We are free?" I say, for the smell of cooking food has reached me and whispers to my heart.

"Quite free," says the woman who brought me to the floor. Her apron has a pattern of red checks. I imagine her at a table, knocking down the dough.

My aunt shakes the man's hand and then the woman's. I copy her, my skin tingling at the touch of another living being.

"Go out through the back," the woman says. She leads us to a door and out into a stairwell. The smell of boiled cabbage hangs heavy in the air. My stomach rumbles. The man pushes past us, down the stairs. The woman stays at the top, apron twisting in her hands. I follow Auntie deeper into darkness. A key turns in a lock. The man holds the door ajar. I breathe in long-forgotten scents, of rain on earth and dusty pavements. I look up at the woman but she has gone. The man presses an apple and a hard bread roll into my hand. The door closes and we step into the night.

I eat the roll and apple without noticing they are gone. We walk for a long time in streets I do not recognise. My aunt turns in and out of alleyways on a route that is known to her alone. Rain seeps into my raincoat collar. The few people whom we pass have hats pulled low and do not look at us.

"We are free, Auntie?" I ask, when my legs begin to ache. Hers must be hurting too, for though we have done our squats each morning, we are not used to exercise.

"Yes, Elli," she replies.

We reach a place where there are shops, their shutters tightly closed. Just one is left un-shuttered. I pause before its window. Amongst the shadows, a faint beam of golden light alights on curving shapes of wood and brass. Joy leaps. I see a trumpet laid out in its case; a pile of banjos; and, in the centre of them all, a cello, as taut and poised as a gazelle.

Auntie pulls my hand. "Do not stop," she hisses.

I stand, rooted, before this cornucopia. It is everything I have dreamed of, in the months I have been shut away.

"Elli!" She is dragging me now, down a passage beside the shop. Rain drips from a gutter. Water splashes in my shoe. There is a door and Auntie knocks on it: *eins, zwei, drei.*

The door edges open and she pushes me inside. I enter, relieved to feel her quick warm breath behind. A man appears before us. He is thin, with small round glasses that have no frames. His hair is brown and slicked back from his forehead. He does not speak but leads us down some stairs into a cellar. Damp taints the air and wooden boxes lie around. I shrink against my aunt but her firm hands send me forward.

"Go, child," she says. And then, more gently: "It is your father."

My father? I know she does not tell the truth. My father is a figure from a fairy tale, as unreal as the Valkyrie that sweeps across the sky. It cannot be my father for, as my mother always told me, my father does not exist.

I turn to my aunt to tell her this but she is closed to me; not my auntie, who sometimes lets me win at chess, but as remote and unreachable as if she has crossed the furthest ocean. Still, this is not my father. I am eight years old. Every fibre tells me I know nothing of this man.

"Elena," he says, as though only to himself.

My head lifts, for it is a long time since I have heard my name. His brown eyes through the small round glasses look at me with hunger. I sense in him a longing little different from the one I feel myself: for my mother, and my books and toys, and everything that went before. I think of the instruments, laid out in his shop window. Is this the man my mother loved: the maker of the cello?

My bow, lost in the life I left behind, leaps back to my hand. Sweet notes tumble as I caress my cello's strings. Perhaps he hears them too, for he smiles. Unwilling, I step towards him. He is our deserter, and my benefactor too. Betrayer of my mother. Sender of the half-sized cello that was mine.

"Papi?" I say.

He takes me in his arms. The tang of old tobacco rises from his jacket. The cello's music lifts and falls. Auntie looks away. I know he will not help us.

AUSCHWITZ II-BIRKENAU, APRIL 1943

The queue of naked girls snakes behind me. I am herded with the other girls and women on to a ramp that leads up to a wooden building. The concrete floor is stained and rough against my feet. A girl beside me whimpers. As instructed, I take off my clothes. The woman up ahead yawns as though in boredom. At last it is my turn to stand before her. My skin is pale, my stomach slicing inwards beneath my ribs. My tiny breasts rise up like buds.

"Were you a teacher?" I say, as the woman twists me round.

"How can you tell?" She is surprised that I should speak.

"My mother was a teacher."

"And now?"

"She died. Before all this." The woman's eyebrows lift, as though to say: she was lucky, in her way. "My aunt is in the camp," I add. "In another section. I will see her soon."

"And you?" the woman says roughly. "What do you do?"

It is a hard question. I have done nothing for a long time, shut up in that attic room. Shut up in a stinking freight car. Shut up in the camp. Once, I had a little dog who liked to lick my hands. Once, I liked to read.

It is evening and the sun is setting. A shaft of light breaks through the narrow window, shining on the wall. I think of the faint glow, falling on the instruments inside my father's shop.

"I play the cello," I remember.

"The cello. Do you hear that, Hanna?" The woman spins me round to face her companion. "This one plays the cello."

"Tell the guard," the woman answers, offhand, for she has her own line of girls to attend to.

My questioner turns me back. "You play well?"

"Yes," I say, in honour of my mother, who played the cello as the swifts and swallows fly, soaring in ever-changing shapes across the sky.

A thud, as something hits my stomach. Overalls. I take them, uncertain.

The woman gestures me away. "Put them on. Play well, if you get the chance."

KONZERTHAUS, BERLIN, 1995

Tonight, as on so many nights, I walk on stage. My long skirt sweeps the shining floor. I wear black, of course; sequins scattered here and there. The touch of my bow is sure, though my old flesh sags. Tonight, as on so many nights, I know that I am loved.

I had my chance and grasped it, more firmly than my captors could have guessed. Fifty years on, I am alive; although, more and more, my thoughts drift back to other times. Where are my paper dolls? My metal sheep and cows? Sometimes I glimpse them, piled up in the past, lost among the bones.

When the worst of it was over, I tried to find my father. He had not suffered, as we had. He was gone nonetheless, run over by a tram. And Auntie? She had been sent the other way, at the camp, when we first got off the train. That was how I pictured her, once I knew the truth: her sturdy stockinged legs protruding from a pile of mangled limbs. A vast and ugly pile that, as time went on, people began to say was never there.

Never there? It haunts my sleep. Never there? I see and breathe and smell it, each night in my dreams.

Applause breaks out. My arm lifts in acknowledgement, then falls back to my side. The crowd gets to its feet. I smile and nod, as they expect.

I tell my story freely now, to those who care to listen. A small tale among so many, but I repeat it all the same. I tell it for the past and for the future; for those who died and those who somehow lived. All of us are but children in the face of history.

The voice comes to me often now, unbidden.

"Pack away now, Elli," it commands, just as my aunt did long ago. "Pack away, for the time to play is over."

Over, when my cello is in my hand, and so much remains to do?

Arbeit macht frei, I answer back, and the voice goes quiet and falls away. For truly, I am free.

ACKNOWLEDGEMENTS

To begin at the beginning, I'd like to thank my mother, a voracious reader, for inspiring my love of books.

Every writer needs encouragement, and I'm extremely grateful to the historical author Joanna Foat for her wisdom, kindness and rigorous reading of my work.

I'm also indebted to the generous and talented writers at Stella Stocker's gently enabling creative writing class at the Guildford Institute.

My husband Roger is often a first reader of my work, and I'm very grateful for his perceptive comments. I'm also inspired every day by the energy and zest for life of my teenage sons. Will and Toby, thank you.

My path to publication has come from entering competitions. I'd very much like to thank the hard-working individuals who run and judge such competitions, and found merit in my work:

The Race, winner of the Historical Writers' Association Dorothy Dunnett Short Story Competition, 2020. Published in the HWA/Dorothy Dunnett short story anthology, 2020.

Becoming Your Best You, as French Tart, longlisted for the Exeter Short Story Prize, 2022

Incident on the Line, winner of the Wells Festival of Literature short story competition, 2021. Published on the Wells Festival website.

Tide Change at the No-Eye-Contact Café, runner-up in the RNA's Elizabeth Goudge trophy, 2022.

Here's To You, Mrs Avery, shortlisted in the Bournemouth Writing Prize, 2021. Published in 'The Waves of Change' and 'Descent', by Fresher Publishing, 2021. An early version of this story was shortlisted in the Harper's Bazaar Short Story Competition, 2018.

Jack's Hedge, winner of the Surrey Wildlife Trust 'Cutting Hedge Creativity' multimedia competition. Published in Surrey Wildlife Trust magazine, autumn 2021.

The Truth Has Arms and Legs, shortlisted in the Harper's Bazaar Short Story Competition, 2019. Longlisted in the Historical Writers' Association/Dorothy Dunnett Short Story Competition, 2019.

Finally, the biggest of thanks to Isabelle Kenyon and Fly On The Wall Press, for bringing my collection to life.

ABOUT THE AUTHOR

Alice Fowler is drawn to writing about outsiders: people at the edges of society. Landscape and the natural world are powerful sources of inspiration. She enjoys how, in the short story form, complex threads can be unpicked and rewoven, within a relatively small word count.

Alice has a degree in Human Sciences from Lady Margaret Hall, Oxford. She worked as a journalist until 2006, writing features and interviews. Her short stories have won and been shortlisted in prizes and printed in anthologies.

She lives in Surrey with her husband and teenage sons. She is passionate about environmental issues, loves theatre, walking and playing tennis, and finds most writerly conundrums can be solved while out walking with her rescue lurcher dog.
www.alicefowlerauthor.com

@alicefwrites
(Twitter)

About Fly on the Wall Press

A publisher with a conscience.
Political, Sustainable, Ethical.
Publishing politically-engaged, international fiction, poetry and cross-genre anthologies on pressing issues. Founded in 2018 by Isabelle Kenyon.

Some other publications:

The Sound of the Earth Singing to Herself by Ricky Ray

We Saw It All Happen by Julian Bishop

Odd as F*ck by Anne Walsh Donnelly

Imperfect Beginnings by Viv Fogel

These Mothers of Gods by Rachel Bower

Fauna by David Hartley

How To Bring Him Back by Clare HM

No One Has Any Intention of Building A Wall by Ruth Brandt

Snapshots of the Apocalypse by Katy Wimhurst

Demos Rising

The House with Two Letterboxes by Janet H Swinney

The State of Us by Charlie Hill

@fly_press (Twitter)
@flyonthewallpress (Instagram and Facebook)
www.flyonthewallpress.co.uk